CHRONICLES ABROAD

Prague

CHRONICLES ABROAD

Prague

Edited by John and Kirsten Miller

CHRONICLE BOOKS
SAN FRANCISCO

Printed in Singapore.

Library of Congress Cataloging-in-Publication Data
Prague / edited by John and Kirsten Miller.
    p. cm.   (Chronicles Abroad)
A collection of previously published literary works and excerpts.
Contents: Article 202 / Vaclav Havel — The castle / Franz Kafka —
Utz / Bruce Chatwin — The house of Doctor Faust / Alois Jirasek
— Bohemia / Ingeborg Bachmann — Pirates / Josef Skvorecky — A
night in Prague / Janet Malcolm — The good soldier Schweik /
Jaroslav Hasek — Freedom at a price / Rosemary Kavan — The
book of laughter and forgetting / Milan Kundera.
ISBN 0-8118-0649-9
1. Prague (Czech Republic)—Literary collections. I. Miller, John,
    1959- . II. Miller, Kirsten, 1963- . III. Series.
Pn6071.p617p73   1994
808.8'03243712—dc20

93-48953
CIP

Editing and design: Big Fish Books
Composition: Jennifer Petersen, Big Fish Books

Distributed in Canada by Raincoast Books,
112 East Third Avenue, Vancouver, B.C. V5T 1C8

10 9 8 7 6 5 4 3 2 1

Chronicle Books
275 Fifth Street
San Francisco, CA 94103

Special thanks to Maggie dePagter

Contents

Patricia Hampl

EPIGRAPH

ECLECTIC, ACCUMULATED, POST-MODERN Prague matches the darting contemporary eye with its own restless moves. It is a walker's city, and on any stroll offers a casual disarray of snapshots of itself: the pock-marked headstones crammed together in the Old Jewish Cemetery, just a block from the new Dior boutique on Art Nouveau Parizska Street; the dark interior of the Old-New Synagogue, begun in the 13th century and said to be the

Novelist Patricia Hampl is the author of Virgin Time. *This excerpt comes from an article entitled* Reflections on a Golden City, *which appeared in* The New York Times Magazine *in 1993.*

oldest functioning synagogue in Europe, with its cave-like vestibules for women to observe the services; a stone pedestrian tunnel along the embankment of Old Town that opens to the surprise of a floating cafe on the river; Gothic Saint Jacob's church where, high above its Baroque heavenscapes, a medieval trophy is displayed as a warning: the decomposed arm of a thief, hanging there on the west wall for more than 400 years.

The city's shoe box full of old snapshots and new takes seems bottomless: the sweeping, impressionistic view from the funicular ride up the slant of Petrin Hill, looking northeast across historic Prague all the way to the grainy black-and-white Communist-era high-rises ranked against the sky like a bleak modern fortress wall; on the Charles Bridge, in fresh focus, an old man playing blues violin next to a grinning boy-entrepreneur bearing a hand-printed sign—"Take your picture with my pretty snake, 30 crowns"—a boa rippling over his shoulders.

And when you're through looking at these, the city seems to say, there's a bunch more somewhere around here. But no rush.

Vaclav Havel

ARTICLE 202

IT WAS MIDNIGHT on a Sunday, and two friends and I were looking for a place in Prague where we could have a glass of wine. Oddly enough, we found one that was not only open, and on Sunday, but it was open until one o'clock. The door was locked, which was not unusual, so we rang the bell. Nothing happened. After a short

Playwright Vaclav Havel was instrumental in the cultural movement leading to the 1968 Prague Spring. Twenty-one years later, when the Soviet control over Czechoslovakia dissolved, Havel, the symbol of Czech spirit, was elected President. "Article 202" is from Open Letters, *a 1991 collection of Havel's writings.*

pause, we rang again. Again, nothing happened. After a longer pause this time, we knocked politely. Still nothing happened. Just as we were about to walk away, the door suddenly opened, not for us, of course, but because the headwaiter was letting one of his friends out. Seizing the opportunity, we asked him, politely, if there might not be room for us inside. Without even bothering to tell us that he was full, or that he didn't want any more customers, or that he was letting only his friends in, in fact, without so much as a reply or a shake of his head or even a glance, the headwaiter simply slammed the door in our faces.

So far, there is nothing unusual in this story: such things happen every night in Prague outside the doors of the few pubs and wine bars left for the use of ordinary citizens.

What is unusual is what happened next: I lost my temper. If I say it's unusual, that's because I'm not at all a short-tempered person, and I rarely have the kind of

tantrums in which the world goes dark before my eyes
and I'm capable of doing things I would never normally
do; if they happen at all, then at the most only once
every seven to ten years. When they do occur, such
tantrums are never provoked by anything important, like
being arrested, or insulted, or having my flat confiscated;
the cause is always something petty. (Once, in the army,
a Private Ulver tripped me as a joke, and I suddenly
found myself pounding him.) In that sense, my tantrum
in front of the wine bar was entirely consistent with my
personal tradition.

I don't exclude the possibility that the petty things
that so anger me may often be merely substitutes for the
big things that don't seem to upset me. Perhaps somewhere in the basement of my calm soul a mysterious battery is slowly charging, and when the potential of this
secretly accumulated exasperation reaches a certain level,
the first petty irritation suddenly causes the entire charge

to be released for what seem to be utterly inappropriate reasons. And Ulver, the innocent practical joker, is cruelly punished because I have had to spend two years building pontoon bridges and taking them down again.

So I lost my temper and began furiously kicking the door of the wine bar. (Oddly enough, there was no damage; the door was obviously made of thick glass.) Naturally, my behavior was absurd and reprehensible; I was behaving like a hooligan. My rational mind knew this, but at that moment, it was not in control.

The wine bar door was probably playing the same role that Private Ulver had played years before. It was being kicked for all the disparagement, the contempt, the humiliation, the rudeness and lack of respect that are, more and more, the daily lot of anonymous man on his journey through life. It was kicked for all that time spent waiting in offices, standing in line at the store, for all the institutions that never answer polite letters, for all the ordinary policemen who can no longer talk to a citizen except as an officer to his batboy, for all that strange conspiracy of finks and informers and black marketeers who have managed to drive the once innocent gaiety out of Prague nightlife. It was probably even kicked for those fellows who kicked Ladislav Hejdánek, or twisted the arms of the Tomín children on the staircase of the apartment block where the Uhls live. It was kicked for all the contemptuous disdain of officials and the fearful timidity of those who are not, a disdain and a timidity that are slowly but surely invading every aspect of life and dehumanizing all manner of living relationships and environments. It was, in short, the outburst of a helpless man who has projected into this minor indignity all the large and complex indignities that surround his life.

None of this, of course, excuses my violent act. On the contrary, it was no way to deal with the whole situation; I was merely succumbing to it. But people are not superhuman and it's no surprise that they occasionally snap. Especially when something is always making them tense.

What followed is not at all surprising: the headwaiter (a mountain of a man) ran into the street, caught me by the collar and, with the help of a friend, dragged me into the wine bar, where both of them began to beat me, yelling at me as they did so that I was a filthy son-of-a-bitch and that they would call the police, who would kick my teeth in. Because my anger had long since been discharged, I behaved realistically, that is to say, like a coward: I did not defend myself. I have my realism to thank for the fact that they soon grew tired of hitting me, and threw me back out into the street. I had gotten off without serious harm being done. My rather rash protest against a minor humiliation (that the waiter had ignored our request) had no serious consequences only because I had silently endured a greater humiliation (allowing myself to be beaten).

But what would have happened had I acted like a man and defended myself?

1. In the first place, I would have paid the tax that is usually paid for such manliness: I would have lost an ear and several teeth, I would have had a broken nose and an arm, two black eyes, and blood on my overcoat.

2. A more serious consequence, however, would have been that as the one who started it all by kicking the door, I would probably have been charged and found guilty of disturbing the peace, according to Article 202 of the Criminal Code, which would mean that I'd probably have been given a second conditional sentence (that is, if I weren't sent straight to jail for the sum of both sentences, with the added advantage, for them, that this time, I wouldn't be a "political" prisoner).

3. An article would appear in the Prague *Evening News* about an incident in front of a wine bar involving the

great human rights activist.

4. A lot of circumspect people would say it was my own fault for behaving like a hooligan.

None of that happened. But I realized that Article 202 is lurking out there every step of the way and that, moreover, it has established its own diplomatic mission inside each one of us. I also realized how this paragraph can entangle a temperamental person in a vicious circle.

Observe the following:

1. Phase one: the spread of humiliation throughout society creates the conditions in which someone like that is bound to lose his temper one day and create a minor "disturbance."

2. As soon as that happens, he can be subjected, by those who have humiliated him, to a new and far deeper humiliation, and, if he is incapable of responding "realis-

tically," as I was, he will defend himself. Once he does so, however, he commits a far more serious "disturbance of the peace," perhaps even "assault on a peace officer."

3. Regardless of how he is punished, humiliation triumphs once more, this time the worst kind of all. If a truly temperamental person is involved, he will thus find himself well on the way to committing some kind of super-disturbance, the consequences of which don't bear thinking about.

Where does all this end?

Isn't the specter of this vicious circle one of the ways to induce in people the required "realism," including the surrender of one's own dignity and honor and the acceptance of what amounts to an official moral commandment: "Don't try to put out a fire that's not burning you"? (A friend of mine was once sentenced for disturbing the peace because he slapped a man who had insulted his girlfriend.)

Everyone knows that people shouldn't slap each other around whenever they feel like it, or kick the doors to wine bars with impunity. And yet there is something about this Article 202 that I find suspect. Not long ago, I talked about it with a lawyer, who told me it was an "import from the East" that has no legal precedent in this country. It is not a political law, but it is the child of a certain way of governing. And in any case, it has some things in common with political laws.

1. It is malleable: essentially anything can be called disturbing the peace if someone declares that it has offended him—a real paradise for informers.

2. The way the article is used depends more than is healthy on the political and spiritual climate. If Ivan Jirous had behaved ten times as eccentrically in 1963 (when he opened the first show of Jiří Laciný's work) as he did in 1977 (when he opened Laciný's most recent

show), it would never have occurred to anyone to arrest him and charge him with disturbing the peace, as they have done now.

3. It may easily be, and often is, used for political repression. Do you need to clap some nonconformist band in jail? Accuse them of disturbing the peace. Do you want to stop a group of young people from meeting at someone's place? Just lock the host up for disturbing the peace; you can always cook up some evidence, and it's easy to find an "outraged" witness. Do you want to make life miserable for a Charter 77 signatory? Just wait until he's had a little too much to drink and is sick in an empty streetcar—and there's your disturbance of the peace. (How many such "disturbers of the peace" could be found in our present political establishment if they were to apply this law in the same way to themselves? Or on the contrary, what would have become of the artistic avant-garde between the wars if Article 202 had existed

then and the bourgeois government of the time had applied it politically in this fashion?)

4. Accusations are made, or not, entirely according to the whims of the authorities. If, for instance, the director of an important Prague factory were to rant and rave on Wenceslas Square and I were to be outraged to the point where I would file a suit against him, the prosecutor's office would merely laugh at it or—which is more probable— they would send my suit straight to Martinovský, who would file it away in the collection of documents he has against me. Whereas if I were the one to rant and rave and the factory director were doing the reporting, I would probably be found guilty of disturbing the peace.

5. It may easily be, and often is, used to settle personal accounts. If Mr. A, who is an enemy of Mr. B, has a good position, all he has to do is say he is outraged by Mr. B's behavior, and Mr. B will find himself saddled with Article 202, when all he may have done is complained about the

boss, or about "conditions," or used a crude word, or dressed differently, or have different habits, sing in the stairwell, or have a dog that barks too loudly.

EVERYTHING INDICATES THAT Article 202 of our Criminal Code was created as one of the countless instruments by which the centralist authorities (originally Czarist, now obviously our own) keep their citizens under permanent control. People may not know very much about the article, but they cannot help but feel it in the air. It is a law that faithfully mirrors a power that is happiest when people don't socialize too much with each other (that is, unless the authorities organize and control it themselves), when they don't go out very often and, when they do go out, always behave quietly, inconspicuously, and with proper humility. It's a power that finds it convenient when people keep an eye on each other, watch each other, are afraid of each other, a power that sees society as an obedient herd whose duty is to be permanently grateful that it has what it has.

I would be interested to know how many people in prison now are there because of Article 202 and what they did to get there. None of them are considered political prisoners and nothing is really known about them. Specific facts about the application of this paragraph might tell us more about conditions in our country and the nature of social power than what we can learn from the known facts about how overtly political laws are applied. What do we know about how many minor expressions of civic discontent have been quickly and easily avenged by this law? About how many personal accounts, masked in a servile loyalty, have been settled? About how many powerless and defenseless people have had their lives ruined for doing something foolish that a powerful person can do with impunity as often as he wants? About how many of those in prison are victims of this application of arbitrary power? And not only that: can it be judged at all how this paragraph has contributed to the leveling, the uniformity, the blandness, and the deadening of life? How it has contributed to the flourishing of informing, to the boom in selfish conformity, to the apathy, the general timidity, and the decline in spontaneous joy of life? How it has become part of the atmosphere of the world in which we live?

I repeat that one should not kick at the door of a wine bar and that every society has the right to defend itself against hooligans and vandals who do that kind of thing. That is one matter.

But this omnipresent, elastic Article 202, which can be used against anyone at any time—especially in *their* hands—that is another matter.

Political trials are a lot of work and make a lot of noise. And people don't really believe in the outcome. Article 202 is much more workable: in the end, who wants to come to the defense of some violent hooligans?

At the same time, the possibilities are limitless: some-day, perhaps, an inconspicuous sneer will be enough, a scarcely audible "hurrah," a moment of suspicious reverie, a different-colored tie.

It's definitely a law with a future.

You might call it the law of the future.

The law of 1984.

At the end of 1977, I was able to get away—barely, and at a rather depressing price—with kicking the door of a wine bar. Would I get away with it this year?

Franz Kafka

THE CASTLE

IT WAS LATE in the evening when K. arrived. The village was deep in snow. The Castle hill was hidden, veiled in mist and darkness, nor was there even a glimmer of light to show that a castle was there. On the wooden bridge leading from the main road to the village, K. stood for a long time gazing into the illusory emptiness above him.

Czech writer Franz Kafka's characters stumble through dizzying mazes peopled by abusive authorities who misjudge, torment, and even kill. The Castle (1926), a classic in this cheery tradition, is set in a misty town that markedly resembles the writer's home—Prague.

Then he went on to find quarters for the night. The inn was still awake, and though the landlord could not provide a room and was upset by such a late and unexpected arrival, he was willing to let K. sleep on a bag of straw in the parlor. K. accepted the offer. Some peasants were still sitting over their beer, but he did not want to talk, and after himself fetching the bag of straw from the attic, he lay down beside the stove. It was a warm corner, the peasants were quiet, and, letting his weary eyes stray over them, he soon fell asleep.

But very shortly he was awakened. A young man dressed like a townsman, with the face of an actor, his eyes narrow and his eyebrows strongly marked, was standing beside him along with the landlord. The peasants were still in the room, and a few had turned their chairs round so as to see and hear better. The young man apologized very courteously for having awakened K., introduced himself as the son of the Castellan, and then said: "This village belongs to the Castle, and whoever lives here or passes the night here does so, in a manner of speaking, in the Castle itself. Nobody may do that without the Count's permission. But you have no such permit, or at least you have produced none."

K. had half raised himself, and now, smoothing down his hair and looking up at the two men, he said: "What village is this I have wandered into? Is there a castle here?"

"Most certainly," replied the young man slowly, while here and there a head was shaken over K.'s remark, "the castle of my lord the Count Westwest."

"And must one have a permit to sleep here?" asked K., as if he wished to assure himself that what he had heard was not a dream.

"One must have a permit," was the reply, and there was an ironical contempt for K. in the young man's gesture as he stretched out his arm and appealed to the others, "Or must one not have a permit?"

"Well, then, I'll have to go and get one," said K., yawning and pushing his blanket away as if to get up.

"And from whom, pray?" asked the young man.

"From the Count," said K., "that's the only thing to be done."

"A permit from the Count in the middle of the night!" cried the young man, stepping back a pace.

"Is that impossible?" inquired K. coolly. "Then why did you waken me?"

At this the young man flew into a passion. "None of your guttersnipe manners!" he cried. "I insist on respect for the Count's authority! I woke you up to inform you that you must quit the Count's territory at once."

"Enough of this fooling," said K. in a markedly quiet voice, laying himself down again and pulling up the blanket. "You're going a little too far, my good fellow, and I'll have something to say tomorrow about your conduct. The landlord here and those other gentlemen will bear me out if necessary. Let me tell you that I am the Land-Surveyor whom the Count is expecting. My assistants are coming on tomorrow in a carriage with the apparatus. I did not want to miss the chance of a walk through the snow, but unfortunately lost my way several times and so arrived very late. That it was too late to present myself at the Castle I knew very well before you saw fit to inform me. That is why I have made shift with this bed for the night, where, to put it mildly, you have had the discourtesy to disturb me. That is all I have to say. Good night, gentlemen." And K. turned over on his side toward the stove.

"Land-Surveyor?" he heard the hesitating question behind his back, and then there was a general silence. But the young man soon recovered his assurance and, lowering his voice sufficiently to appear considerate of K.'s sleep while yet speaking loud enough to be clearly heard, said to the landlord: "I'll ring up and inquire." So there was a telephone in this village inn? They had everything up to the mark. The particular instance surprised K., but on the whole he had really expected it. It appeared that the telephone was placed almost over his head, and in his drowsy condition he had overlooked it. If the young man must telephone, he could not, even with the best intentions, avoid disturbing K. The only question was whether K. would let him do so; he decided to allow it. In that case, however, there was no sense in pretending to sleep, and so he turned on his back again. He could see the peasants putting their heads together; the arrival of a land-surveyor was no small event. The door in the kitchen had been opened, and blocking the whole doorway stood the imposing figure of the landlady, to whom the landlord was advancing on tiptoe in order to tell her what was happening. And now the conversation began on the telephone. The Castellan was asleep, but an under-castellan, one of the under-castellans, a certain Herr Fritz, was available. The young man, announcing himself as Schwarzer, reported that he had found K., a disreputable-looking man in his thirties, sleeping calmly on a bag of straw with a minute rucksack for pillow and a knotty stick within reach. He had naturally suspected the fellow, and as the landlord had obviously neglected his duty, he, Schwarzer, had felt bound to investigate the matter. He had roused the man, questioned him, and duly warned him off the Count's territory, all of which K. had taken with an ill grace, perhaps with some justification, as it eventually turned out, for he claimed to be a land-surveyor engaged by the Count. Of course, to say the least of it, that was a statement which required official confirmation, and so Schwarzer begged Herr Fritz to inquire in the Central Bureau if a land-surveyor was really expected, and to telephone the answer at once.

Then there was silence while Fritz was making inquiries up there and the young man was waiting for the answer. K. did not change his position, did not even once turn round, seemed quite indifferent, and stared into space. Schwarzer's report, in its combination of malice and prudence, gave him an idea of the measure of diplomacy in which even underlings in the Castle, like Schwarzer, were versed. Nor were they remiss in industry: the Central Office had a night service. And apparently answered questions quickly, too, for Fritz was already ringing. His reply seemed brief enough, for Schwarzer hung ·up the receiver immediately, crying angrily: "Just what I said! Not a trace of a land-surveyor. A common, lying tramp, and probably worse." For a moment K. thought that all of them— Schwarzer, the peasants, the landlord, and the landlady— were going to fall upon him in a body, and to escape at least the first shock of their assault he crawled right underneath the blanket. But the telephone rang again, and with a special insistence, it seemed to K. Slowly he put out his head. Although it was improbable that this message also concerned K., they all stopped short and Schwarzer took up the receiver once more. He listened to a fairly long statement, and then said in a low voice: "A mistake, is it? I'm sorry to hear that. The head of the department himself said so? Very queer, very queer. How am I to explain it all to the Land-Surveyor?"

K. pricked up his ears. So the Castle had recognized him as the Land-Surveyor. That was unpropitious for him, on the one hand, for it meant that the Castle was well informed about him, had estimated all the probable chances, and was taking up the challenge with a smile. On the other hand, however, it was quite propitious, for if his interpretation was right they had underestimated his strength, and he would have more freedom of action than he had dared to hope. And if they expected to cow him by their lofty superiority in recognizing him as Land-Surveyor, they were mistaken; it made his skin prickle a little, that was all.

He waved off Schwarzer, who was timidly approaching him, and refused an urgent invitation to transfer himself into the landlord's own room; he only accepted a warm drink from the landlord, and from the landlady a basin to wash in, a piece of soap, and a towel. He did not even have to ask that the room should be cleared, for all the men flocked out with averted faces lest he should recognize them again next day. The lamp was blown out, and he was left in peace at last. He slept deeply until morning, scarcely disturbed by rats scuttling past once or twice.

After breakfast, which, according to his host, was to be paid for by the Castle, together with all the other expenses of his board and lodging, he prepared to go out immediately into the village. But as the landlord, to whom he had been very curt because of his behavior the preceding night, kept circling around him in dumb entreaty, he took pity on the man and asked him to sit down for a while.

"I haven't met the Count yet," said K., "but he pays well for good work, doesn't he? When a man like me travels so far from home, he wants to go back with something in his pockets."

"There's no need for the gentleman to worry about that kind of thing; nobody complains of being badly paid."

"Well," said K., "I'm not one of your timid people, and can give a piece of my mind even to a count, but of course it's much better to have everything settled without any trouble."

The landlord sat opposite K. on the rim of the window-seat, not daring to take a more comfortable place, and kept on gazing at K. with an anxious look in his large brown eyes. He had thrust his company on K. at first, but now it seemed that he was eager to escape. Was he afraid of being cross-questioned about the Count? Was he afraid of some indiscretion on the part of the "gentleman" whom he took K. to be? K. must divert his attention. He looked at the clock and said: "My assistants should be arriving soon. Will you be able to put them up here?"

"Certainly, sir," he said, "but won't they be staying with you up at the Castle?"

Was the landlord so willing, then, to give up prospective customers, and K. in particular, whom he so unconditionally transferred to the Castle?

"That's not at all certain yet," said K.; "I must first find out what work I am expected to do. If I have to work down here, for instance, it would be more sensible to lodge down here. I'm afraid, too, that the life in the Castle wouldn't suit me. I like to be my own master."

"You don't know the Castle," said the landlord quietly.

"Of course," replied K., "one shouldn't judge prematurely. All that I know at present about the Castle is that the people there know how to choose a good land-surveyor. Perhaps it has other attractions as well." And he stood up in order to rid the landlord of his presence, for the man was biting his lip uneasily. His confidence was not to be lightly won.

As K. was going out, he noticed a dark portrait in a dim frame on the wall. He had already observed it from his couch by the stove, but from that distance he had not been able to distinguish any details and had thought that it was only a plain back to the frame. But it was a picture after all, as now appeared, the bust portrait of a man about fifty. His head was sunk so low upon his breast that his eyes were scarcely visible, and the weight of the high, heavy forehead and the strong hooked nose seemed to have borne the head down. Because of this pose the man's full beard was pressed in at the chin and spread out farther down. His left hand was buried in his luxuriant hair, but seemed incapable of supporting the head. "Who is that?" asked K.; "the Count?" He was standing before the portrait and did not look round at the landlord. "No," said the latter, "the Castellan." "A handsome castellan, indeed," said K.; "a pity that he has such an ill-bred son." "No, no," said the landlord, drawing K. a little toward him and whispering in his hear: "Schwarzer exaggerated yesterday; his father is only an under-castellan, and one of the lowest, too." At that moment the landlord struck K. as a very child. "The villain!" said K. with a laugh. But the landlord instead of laughing said: "Even his father is powerful." "Get along with you," said K., "you think everyone powerful. Me too, perhaps?" "No," he replied, timidly yet seriously, "I don't think you powerful." "You're a keen observer," said K., "for between you and me I'm not really powerful. And consequently I suppose I have no less respect for the powerful than you have, only I'm not so honest as you and am not always willing to acknowledge it." And K. gave the landlord a tap on the cheek to hearten him and awaken his friendliness. It made the man smile a little. He was actually young, with that soft and almost beardless face of his; how had he come to have that massive, elderly wife, who could be seen through a small window bustling about the kitchen with her elbows sticking out? K. did not want to force his confidence any farther, however, nor to scare away the smile he had at last evoked. So he only signed to him to open the door, and went out into the brilliant winter morning.

Now he could see the Castle above him, clearly defined in the glittering air, its outline made still more definite by the thin layer of snow covering everything. There seemed to be much less snow up there on the hill than down in the village, where K. found progress as laborious as on the main road the previous day. Here the heavy snowdrifts reached right up to the cottage windows and began again on the low roofs, but up on the hill everything soared light and free into the air, or at least so it appeared from below.

On the whole this distant prospect of the Castle satisfied K.'s expectations. It was neither an old stronghold nor a new mansion, but a rambling pile consisting of innumerable small buildings closely packed together and of one or two stories; if K. had not known that it was a castle he might have taken it for a little town. There was only one tower as far as he could see; whether it belonged to a dwelling-house or a church he could not determine. Swarms of crows were circling round it.

With his eyes fixed on the Castle, K. went on farther, thinking of nothing else at all. But on approaching it he was disappointed in the Castle; it was after all only a wretched-looking town, a huddle of village houses, whose sole merit, if any, lay in being built of stone; but the plaster had long since flaked off and the stone seemed to be crumbling away. K. had a fleeting recollection of his native town. It was hardly inferior to this so-called Castle, and if it was merely a question of enjoying the view, it was a pity to have come so far; K. would have done better to revisit his native town, which he had not seen for such a long time. And in his mind he compared the church tower at home with the tower above him. The church tower, firm in line, soaring unfalteringly to its tapering point, topped with red tiles and broad in the roof, an earthly building—what else can men build?—but with a loftier goal than the humble dwelling-houses, and a clearer meaning than the muddle of everyday life. The tower above him here—the only one visible—the tower of a house, as was now evident, perhaps of the main building, was uniformly round, part of it graciously mantled with ivy, pierced by small windows that glittered in the sun—with a somewhat maniacal glitter—and topped by what looked like an attic, with battlements that were irregular, broken, fumbling, as if designed by the trembling or careless hand of a child, clearly outlined against the blue. It was as if a melancholy-mad tenant who ought to have been kept locked in the topmost chamber of his house had burst through the roof and lifted himself up to the gaze of the world.

Again K. came to a stop, as if in standing still he had more power of judgment. But he was disturbed. Behind the village church where he had stopped—it was really only a chapel widened with barnlike additions so as to accommodate the parishioners—was the school. A long, low building, combining remarkably a look of great age with a provisional appearance, it lay behind a fenced-in garden, which was now a field of snow. The children were just coming out with their teacher. They thronged around him, all gazing up at him and chattering without a break so rapidly that K. could not follow what they said. The teacher, a small young man with narrow shoulders and a very upright carriage, which yet did not make him ridiculous, had already fixed K. with his eyes from the distance, naturally enough, for apart from the school-children there was not another human being in sight. Being the stranger, K. made the first advance, especially as the other was such an authoritative-looking little man, and said: "Good morning, sir." As if by one accord the children fell silent; perhaps the master liked to have a sudden stillness as a preparation for his words. "You are looking at the Castle?" he asked more gently than K. had expected, but with an inflection that denoted disapproval of K.'s occupation. "Yes," said K. "I am a stranger here, I came to the village only last night." "You don't like the Castle?" asked the teacher quickly. "What?" countered K., a little taken aback, and repeated the question in a modified form. "Do I like the Castle? Why do you assume that I don't like it?" "Strangers never do," said the teacher. To avoid saying the wrong thing, K. changed the subject and asked: "I suppose you know the Count?" "No," said the teacher, turning away. But K. would not be put off and asked again: "What, you don't know the Count?" "Why should I?" replied the teacher in a low tone, and added aloud in

French: "Please remember that there are innocent children present." K. took this as a justification for asking: "Might I come to pay you a visit some day, sir? I am to be staying here for some time and already feel a little lonely. I don't fit in with the peasants, nor, I imagine, with the Castle." "There is no difference between the peasantry and the Castle," said the teacher. "Maybe," said K., "that doesn't alter my position. Can I pay you a visit some day?" "I live in Swan Street at the butcher's." That was assuredly more of a statement than an invitation, but K. said: "Right, I'll come." The teacher nodded and moved on with his batch of children, who immediately began to scream again. They soon vanished in a steeply descending bystreet.

But K. was disconcerted, irritated by the conversation. For the first time since his arrival he felt really tired. The long journey he had made seemed at first to have imposed no strain upon him—how quietly he had sauntered

through the days, step by step!——but now the consequences of his exertion were making themselves felt, and
at the wrong time, too. He felt irresistibly drawn to seek
out new acquaintances, but each new acquaintance only
seemed to increase his weariness. If he forced himself in
his present condition to go on at least as far as the Castle
entrance, he would have done more than enough.

So he resumed his walk, but the way proved long.
For the street he was in, the main street of the village, did
not lead up to the Castle hill; it only made toward it and
then, as if deliberately, turned aside, and though it did not
lead away from the Castle, it led no nearer to it either. At
every turn K. expected the road to double back to the
Castle, and only because of this expectation did he go on;
he was flatly unwilling, tired as he was, to leave the street,
and he was also amazed at the length of the village, which
seemed to have no end——again and again the same little
houses and frost-bound windowpanes and snow and the

entire absence of human beings—but at last he tore himself away from the obsession of the street and escaped into a small side-lane, where the snow was still deeper and the exertion of lifting one's feet clear was fatiguing; he broke into a sweat, suddenly came to a stop, and could not go on.

Well, he was not on a desert island; there were cottages to right and left of him. He made a snowball and threw it at a window. The door opened immediately—the first door that had opened during the whole length of the village—and there appeared an old peasant in a brown fur jacket, with his head cocked to one side, a frail and kindly figure. "May I come into your house for a little?" asked K.; "I'm very tired." He did not hear the old man's reply, but thankfully observed that a plank was pushed out toward him to rescue him from the snow, and in a few steps he was in the kitchen.

A large kitchen, dimly lit. Anyone coming in from

outside could make out nothing at first. K. stumbled over a washtub; a woman's hand steadied him. The crying of children came loudly from one corner. From another, steam was welling out and turning the dim light into darkness. K. stood as if in the clouds. "He must be drunk," said somebody. "Who are you?" cried a hectoring voice, and then obviously to the old man: "Why did you let him in? Are we to let in everybody who wanders about in the street?" "I am the Count's Land-Surveyor," said K., trying to justify himself before this still invisible personage. "Oh, it's the Land-Surveyor," said a woman's voice, and then came a complete silence. "You know me, then?" asked K. "Of course," said the same voice curtly. The fact that he was known did not seem to be a recommendation.

At last the steam thinned a little, and K. was able gradually to make things out. It seemed to be a general wash-day. Near the door clothes were being washed. But the steam was coming from another corner, where in a wooden tub larger than any K. had ever seen, as wide as two beds, two men were bathing in steaming water. But still more astonishing, though one could not say what was so astonishing about it, was the scene in the right-hand corner. From a large opening, the only one in the back wall, a pale snowy light came in, apparently from the courtyard, and gave a gleam as of silk to the dress of a woman who was almost reclining in a high arm-chair. She was suckling an infant at her breast. Several children were playing around her, peasant children, as was obvious, but she seemed to be of another class, though of course illness and weariness give even peasants a look of refinement.

"Sit down!" said one of the men, who had a full beard and breathed heavily through his mouth, which always hung open, pointing—it was a funny sight—with his wet hand over the edge of the tub toward a settle, and showering drops of warm water all over K.'s face as he did so. On the settle the old man who had admitted K. was already sitting, sunk in vacancy. K. was thankful to find a seat at last. Nobody paid any further attention to him. The woman at the washtub, young, plump, and fair, sang in a low voice as she worked; the men stamped and rolled about in the bath; the children tried to get closer to them, but were constantly driven back by mighty splashes of water, which fell on K., too; and the woman in the armchair lay as if lifeless, staring at the roof without even a glance toward the child at her bosom.

She made a beautiful, sad, fixed picture, and K. looked at her for what must have been a long time; then he must have fallen asleep, for when a loud voice roused him, he found that his head was lying on the old man's shoulder. The men had finished with the tub—in which the children were now wallowing in charge of the fair-haired woman—and were standing fully dressed before K. It appeared that the hectoring one with the full beard was the less important of the two. The other, a quiet, slow-thinking man who kept his head bent, was not taller than his companion and had a much smaller beard, but he was broader in the shoulders and had a broad face as well, and he it was who said: "You can't stay here, sir. Excuse the discourtesy." "I don't want to stay," said K.; "I only wanted to rest a little. I have rested, and now I shall go." "You're probably surprised at our lack of hospitality," said the man, "but hospitality is not our custom here; we have no use for visitors." Somewhat refreshed by his sleep, his perceptions somewhat quickened, K. was pleased by the man's frankness. He felt less constrained, poked with his stick here and there, approached the woman in the armchair, and noted that he himself was physically the biggest man in the room.

"To be sure," said K.; "what use would you have

for visitors? But still you need one now and then—me, for example, the Land-Surveyor." "I don't know about that," replied the man slowly. "If you've been asked to come, you're probably needed; that's an exceptional case; but we small people stick to our tradition, and you can't blame us for that." "No, no," said K., "I am only grateful to you, to you and everybody here." And taking them all by surprise, he made an adroit turn and stood before the reclining woman. Out of weary blue eyes she looked at him. A transparent silk kerchief hung down to the middle of her forehead. The infant was asleep on her bosom. "Who are you?" asked K.; and disdainfully—whether contemptuous of K. or of her own answer was not clear—she replied: "A girl from the Castle."

It had only taken a second or so, but already the two men were at either side of K. and were pushing him toward the door, as if there were no other means of persuasion, silently, but with all their strength. Something in this procedure delighted the old man, and he clapped his hands. The woman at the bathtub laughed too, and the children suddenly shouted like mad.

K. was soon out in the street, and from the threshold the two men surveyed him. Snow was again falling, yet the sky seemed a little brighter. The bearded man cried impatiently: "Where do you want to go? This is the way to the Castle, and that to the village." K. made no reply to him, but turned to the other, who in spite of his shyness seemed to him the more amiable of the two, and said: "Who are you? Whom have I to thank for sheltering me?" "I am the tanner Lasemann," was the answer, "but you owe thanks to nobody." "All right," said K., "perhaps we'll meet again." "I don't suppose so," said the man. At that moment the other cried, with raised hand: "Good morning, Arthur; good morning, Jeremiah!" K. turned round; so there were really people to be seen in the village streets! From the direction of the Castle came two young men of medium height, both very slim, in tight-fitting clothes, and like each other in their features. Although their skin was a dusky brown, the blackness of their little pointed beards was actually striking by contrast. Considering the state of the road, they were walking at a great pace, their slim legs keeping step. "Where are you off to?" shouted the bearded man. One had to shout to them, they were going so fast, and they did not stop. "On business," they shouted back, laughing. "Where?" "At the inn." "I'm going there too," yelled K. suddenly, louder than all the rest; he felt a strong desire to accompany them, not that he expected much from their acquaintance, but because they were obviously good and jolly companions. They heard him, but only nodded and then were out of sight.

K. was still standing in the snow, and was little inclined to extricate his feet only for the sake of plunging them in again. The tanner and his comrade, satisfied with having finally got rid of him, edged slowly into the house through the door, which was now barely ajar, casting backward glances at K., and he was left alone in the falling snow. "A fine setting for a fit of despair," it occurred to him, "if I were only standing here by accident instead of design."

Just then in the hut on his left hand a tiny window was opened, which had seemed quite blue when shut, perhaps from the reflection of the snow, and was so tiny that, when opened, it did not permit the whole face of the person behind it to be seen, but only the eyes, old brown eyes. "There he is," K. heard a woman's trembling voice say. "It's the Land-Surveyor," answered a man's voice. Then the man came to the window and asked, not unamiably, but still as if he were anxious to have no complications in front of his house: "Are you waiting for somebody?" "For a sledge, to pick me up," said K. "No sledges will pass here," said the man, "there's no traffic here." "But it's the road leading to the Castle," objected K. "All the same, all the same," said the man with a certain finality, "there's no traffic here." Then they were both silent. But the man was obviously thinking of something, for he kept the window open. "It's a bad road," said K., to help him out. The only answer he got, however, was: "Oh, yes." But after a little the man volunteered: "If you like, I'll take you in my sledge." "Please do," said K., delighted; "what is your charge?" "Nothing," said the man. K. was much surprised. "Well, you're the Land-Surveyor," explained the man, "and you belong to the Castle. Where do you want to be taken?" "To the Castle," answered K. quickly. "I won't take you there," said the man without hesitation. "But I belong to the Castle," said K., repeating the other's very words. "Maybe," said the man shortly. "Oh, well, take me to the inn," said K. "All right," said the man, "I'll be out with the sledge in a moment." His whole behavior had the appearance of springing not from any special desire to be friendly but rather from a kind of selfish, worried, and almost pedantic insistence on shifting K. away from the front of the house.

The gate of the courtyard opened, and a small, light sledge appeared, quite flat, without a seat of any kind, drawn by a feeble little horse, and behind it limped the man, a weak, stooping figure with a gaunt red snuffling face that looked peculiarly small beneath a tightly wrapped woolen scarf. He was obviously ailing, and yet only to transport K. he had dragged himself out. K. ventured to mention it, but the man waved him aside. All that K. elicited was that he was a coachman called Gerstäcker, and that he had taken this uncomfortable sledge because it was standing ready, and to get out one of the others would have wasted too much time. "Sit down," he said, pointing to the sledge. "I'll sit beside you," said K. "I'm going to walk," said Gerstäcker. "But why?" asked K. "I'm going to walk," repeated Gerstäcker, and was seized with a fit of coughing which shook him so severely that he had to brace his legs in the snow and hold on to the rim of the sledge. K. said no more, but sat down on the sledge, the man's cough slowly abated, and they drove off.

The Castle above them, which K. had hoped to reach that very day, was already beginning to grow dark and retreated again into the distance. But as if to give him a parting sign till their next encounter, a bell began to ring merrily up there, a bell that for at least a second made his heart palpitate, for its tone was menacing, too, as if it threatened him with the fulfillment of his vague desire. This great bell soon died away, however, and its place was taken by a feeble, monotonous little tinkle, which might have come from the Castle, but might have been somewhere in the village. It certainly harmonized better with the slow journey and with the wretched-looking yet inexorable driver.

"I say," cried K. suddenly—they were already near the church, the inn was not far off, and K. felt he could risk something—"I'm surprised that you have the nerve to drive me round on your own responsibility. Are you allowed to do that?" Gerstäcker paid no attention, but went on walking quietly beside the little horse. "Hi!" cried K., scraping some snow from the sledge and flinging a snowball, which hit Gerstäcker full in the ear. That made him stop and turn round; but when K. saw him at such close quarters—the sledge had slid forward a little—this stooping and somehow ill-used figure with the thin, red, tired face and cheeks that were different—one being flat and the other fallen in—standing listening with his mouth open, displaying only a few isolated teeth, he found that what he had just said out of malice had to be repeated out of pity, that is, whether

Gerstäcker was likely to be penalized for driving him. "What do you mean?" asked Gerstäcker uncomprehendingly; but without waiting for an answer he spoke to the horse and they moved on again.

Bruce Chatwin

UTZ

KNOWING NO ONE in Prague, I asked a friend, a historian who specialised in the Iron Curtain countries, if there was anyone he'd recommend me to see.

He replied that Prague was still the most mysterious of European cities, where the supernatural was always a possibility. The Czechs' propensity to "bend" before superior force was not necessarily a weakness. Rather, their

Nomad novelist Bruce Chatwin traveled widely in Asia, Europe, Africa, and the Americas, compiling material for his exotic travel books, In Patagonia, The Viceroy of Ouidah, *and* The Songlines. *This excerpt is from* Utz, *his last novel. Chatwin died in 1989.*

metaphysical view of life encouraged them to look on acts of force as ephemera.

"Of course," he said, "I could send you to any number of intellectuals. Poets, painters, film-makers." Providing I could face an interminable whine about the role of the artist in a totalitarian state, or wished to go to a party that would end in a *partouse*.

I protested. Surely he was exaggerating?

"No," he shook his head. "I don't think so."

He would be the last to denigrate a man who risked the labour camp for publishing a poem in a foreign journal. But, in his view, the true heroes of this impossible situation were people who wouldn't raise a murmur against the Party or State—yet who seemed to carry the sum of Western Civilisation in their heads.

"With their silence," he said, "they inflict a final insult on the State, by pretending it does not exist."

Where else would one find, as he had, a tram-ticket salesman who was a scholar of the Elizabethan stage? Or a street-sweeper who had written a philosophical commentary on the Anaximander Fragment?

He finished by observing that Marx's vision of an age of infinite leisure had, in one sense, come true. The State, in its efforts to wipe out "traces of individualism," offered limitless time for the intelligent individual to dream his private and heretical thoughts.

I said my motive for visiting Prague was perhaps more frivolous than his—and I explained my interest in the Emperor Rudolf.

"In that case I'll send you to Utz," he said. "Utz is a Rudolf of our time."

UTZ AND I spent the afternoon strolling through the thinly peopled streets of Malá Strana, pausing now and then to admire the blistering façade of a merchant's house, or some Baroque or Rococo palace—the Vrtba, the Pálffy, the Lobkovic: he recited their names as though the builders were intimate friends.

In the Church of Our Lady Victorious, the waxen Spanish image of the Christ Child, aureoled in an explosion of gold, seemed less the Blessed Babe of Bethlehem than the vengeful divinity of the Counter-Reformation.

We climbed the length of Neruda Street and walked around the Hradschin: the scene of my futile researches during the previous week. We then sat in an orchard below the Strahov Monastery. A man in his underpants sunned himself on the grass. The fluff of balsam poplars floated by, and settled on our clothes like snowflakes.

"You will see," said Utz, waving his malacca over the multiplicity of porticoes and cupolas below us. "This city wears a tragic mask."

It was also a city of giants: giants in stone, in stucco or marble; naked giants; blackamoor giants; giants dressed as if for a hurricane, not one of them in repose, struggling with some unseen force, or heaving under the weight of architraves.

"The suffering giant," he added without conviction,

"is the emblem of our persecuted people."

I commented facetiously that a taste for giants was usually a symptom of decline: an age that took the Farnese Hercules for an ideal was bound to end in trouble.

Utz countered with the story of Frederick William of Prussia who had once made a collection of real giants— semi-morons mostly—to swell the ranks of his Potsdam Grenadiers.

He then explained how this weakness for giants had led to one of the most bizarre diplomatic transactions of the eighteenth century: in which Augustus of Saxony chose 127 pieces of Chinese porcelain from the Palace of Charlottenburg, in Berlin, and gave in return 600 giants "of the required height" collected in the eastern provinces.

"I never liked giants," he said.

"I once met a man," I said, "who was a dealer in dwarfs."

"Oh?" he blinked. "Dwarfs, you say?"

"Dwarfs."

"Where did you meet this man?"

"On a plane to Baghdad. He was going to view a dwarf for a client."

"A client! This is wonderful!"

"He had two clients," I said. "One was an Arab oil sheikh. The other owned hotels in Pakistan."

"And what did they do with those dwarfs?" Utz tapped me on the knee.

He had paled with excitement and was mopping the sweat from his brow.

"Kept them," I said. "The sheikh, if I remember right, liked to sit his favourite dwarf on his forearm and his favourite falcon on the dwarf's forearm."

"Nothing else?"

"How can one know?"

"You are right," said Utz. "These are things one cannot know."

"Or would want to."

"And what would cost a dwarf? These days?"

"Who can say? Collecting dwarfs has always been expensive."

"That's a nice story," he smiled at me. "Thank you. I also like dwarfs. But not in the way you think."

IT WAS NOW early evening and we were sitting on a slatted seat in the Old Jewish Cemetery. Pigeons were burbling on the roof of the Klausen Synagogue. The sunbeams, falling through sycamores, lit up spirals of midges and landed on the mossy tombstones, which, heaped one upon the other, resembled seaweed-covered rocks at low-tide.

To our right, a party of American Hasids—pale, short-sighted youths in yarmulkes—were laying pebbles on the tomb of the Great Rabbi Loew. They posed for a photograph, with their backs to its scrolling head-stone.

Utz told me how the original ghetto—that warren of

secret passages and forgotten rooms so vividly described by Meyrink—had been replaced by apartment buildings after the slum clearances of the 1890s. The synagogues, the cemetery and the Old Town Hall were almost the only monuments to survive. These, he said, far from being destroyed by the Nazis, were spared to form a proposed Museum of Jewry, where Aryan tourists of the future would inspect the relics of a people as lost as the Aztecs or Hottentots.

He changed the subject.

"You have heard tell the story of the Golem?"

"I have," I said. "The Golem was an artificial man . . . a mechanical man . . . a prototype of the robot. He was a creation of the Rabbi Loew."

"My friend," he smiled, "you know, I think, many things. But you have many things to know."

THE RABBI LOEW had been the undisputed leader of Prague Jewry in the reign of the Emperor Rudolf:

never again would the Jews of Middle Europe enjoy such esteem and privilege. He entertained princes and ambassadors, and was entertained by his sovereign in the Hradschin. Many of his writings—among them the homily "On the Hardening of Pharoh's Heart"—were absorbed into the teachings of Hasidism. Like any other Cabbalist he believed that every event—past, present and future—was already written down in the Torah.

After his death, the Rabbi was inevitably credited with supernatural powers. There are tales—none dating from his lifetime—of how, with an abracadabra, he moved a castle from the Bohemian countryside to the Prague ghetto. Or told the Emperor to his face that his real father was a Jew. Or trounced the mad Jesuit, Father Thaddeus, and proved the Jews were innocent of blood guilt. Or fashioned Yossel the Golem from the glutinous mud of the River Vltava.

All golem legends derived from an Ancient Jewish belief that any righteous man could create the World by repeating, in an order prescribed by the Cabbala, the letters of the secret name of God. "Golem" meant "unformed" or "uncreated" in Hebrew. Father Adam himself had been "golem"—an inert mass of clay so vast as to cover the ends of the Earth: that is, until Yahweh shrank him to human scale and breathed into his mouth the power of speech.

"So you see," said Utz, "not only was Adam the first human person. He was also the first ceramic sculpture."

"Are you suggesting your porcelains are alive?"

"I am and I am not," he said. "They are alive and they are dead. But if they *were* alive, they would also have to die. Is it not?'

"If you say so."

"Good. So I say it."

"Good," I said. "Go on about golems."

One of Utz's favourite golem stories was a mediaeval text discovered by Gershom Scholem: wherein it was written that Jesus Christ ("like *our* friend J. J. Kaendler") used to make model birds from clay—which, once He had uttered the sacred formula, would sing, flap their wings and fly.

A second story ("Oh! What a Jewish story!") told of two hungry rabbis who, having fashioned the figure of a calf, brought it to life—then cut its throat and ate veal for supper.

As for making a golem, a recipe in the Sepher Yetzirah or "Book of Creation" called for a quantity of untouched mountain soil. This was to be kneaded with fresh spring water and, from it, a human image formed. The maker was required to recite over each of the image's limbs the appropriate alphabetical combination. He then walked around it clockwise a number of times: whereupon the golem stood and lived. Were he to reverse the direction, the creature would revert to clay.

None of the earlier sources say whether or not a golem could speak. But the automaton did have the gift of memory and would obey orders mechanically, without reflection, providing these were given at regular intervals.

If not, the golem might run amok.

Golems also gained in stature, inch by inch, every day: yearning, it would seem, to attain the gigantic size of the Cosmic Adam—and so crush their creators and over-whelm the world.

"There was no end," said Utz, "to the size of golems. Golems were highly dangerous."

A golem was said to wear a slip of metal known as the "shem," either across its forehead or under its tongue. The "shem" was inscribed with the Hebrew word "emeth," or Truth of God. When a rabbi wished to destroy his golem, he had only to pluck out the opening letter, so that "emeth" now read "meth"—which is to say "death"—and the golem dissolved.

"I see," I said. "The 'shem' was a kind of battery?"

"It was."

"Without which the machine wouldn't work?"

"Also."

"And the Rabbi Loew . . . ?"

"Wanted a servant. He was a good Jewish business-man. He wanted a servant without paying wages."

"And a servant that wouldn't answer back!"

YOSSEL WAS THE name of the Rabbi Loew's golem. On weekdays he did all sorts of menial tasks. He chopped wood, swept the street and the synagogue, and acted as watchdog in case the Jesuits got up to mischief. Yet on the Sabbath—since all God's creatures must rest on the Sabbath—his master would remove the "shem" and render him lifeless for a day.

One Sabbath the Rabbi forgot to do this, and Yossel went berserk. He pulled down houses, threw rocks, threatened people and tore up trees by the roots. The congregation had already filled the Altneu Synagogue for morning prayers, and was chanting the 92nd Psalm: "My horn shalt thou exalt like the horn of the unicorn . . . " The Rabbi rushed into the street and snatched the "shem" from the monster's forehead.

Another version places the "death," amid old books and prayer-shawls, in the loft of the synagogue.

"Tell me," I asked, "would a golem have had Jewish features?"

"Not!" Utz answered with a touch of impatience. "The golem was always a servant. Servants in Jewish houses were always of the goyim."

"Would a golem have had Nordic features?"

"Yes," he agreed. "Giants' features."

Utz brooded for a while and then arrived at the crux of the discussion:

All these tales suggested that the golem-maker had acquired arcane secrets: yet, in doing so, had transgressed Holy Law. A man-made figure was a blasphemy. A golem, by its presence alone, issued a warning against idolatry— and actively beseeched its own destruction.

"Would you say then," I asked, "that art-collecting is idolatry?"

"Ja! Ja!" he struck his chest. "Of course! Of course! That

is why we Jews . . . and in this matter I consider myself a Jew . . . are so *good* at it! Because it is forbidden . . . ! Because it is sinful . . . ! Because it is dangerous . . . !"

"Do your porcelains demand their own death?"

He stroked his chin.

"I do not know. It is a very problematical question."

The other visitors had left. A black cat had positioned itself on the crest of a tombstone. The guardian told us it was time to leave.

"And now my friend," said Utz, "would it amuse you to see my collection of dwarfs?"

Alois Jirasek

THE HOUSE OF DOCTOR FAUST

THIS ANCIENT HOUSE stood at Skalka, at the end of the Cattle Market, on the corner opposite the Slav monastery. For a long, long time no one had lived in it, and for that reason its appearance was shabby and neglected. The once red roof had darkened, the walls were cracking, the windows filmed over with dust and

---

In the late nineteenth century, Czech writer Alois Jirasek assembled his magical Legends of Bohemia, *a cornucopia of ancient myths, legends, and fables—many of which had been long forgotten. "The House of Doctor Faust" is one of the more colorful from the writer's collection.*

rain were like blind eyes, full of cobwebs. The heavy oak door studded with enormous nails was never opened, nor even the smaller wicket door in it, and nobody stopped at the portal to reach for the graceful wrought-iron knocker.

Within the gate all was silent and deserted; no dog barked there, no cock crowed, and in front of the gate grass grew thick among the cobbles.

No less mournful was the garden behind the house and beside it, along the road directly opposite the Slav cloister. No one took care of it now. It had no flowerbeds, no plots of herbs or vegetables. Even the paths in it had vanished, overgrown with grass. Nothing but grass everywhere, luxuriant, tall grass, smothering even the trunks of the old maples, limes and fruit trees, whose boles and boughs were muffled in lichens and mosses.

Only in spring, when the flowers came, when the thick grass was starred with dandelions like gold coins, and later grew white with goat's-lip and hemlock, did the garden look a little gayer. But in autumn, when the leaves fell and drowned the whole enclosure of the garden, when the sky loomed low and heavy with menace and the wind wailed through the bare branches, and after the early twilight the darkness closed in on the whole house, the place became more dismal than ever!

Melancholy exhaled from garden and house, and a strange dread fell on the people who passed by it. It was an accursed place; in the night the soul of Doctor Faust walked there, unable to find peace after death as he had failed to find it living. For long, long ago Doctor Faust had lived in this house. Here he had cast his magic spells and pored over his books of sorcery, here he called up the devil and signed away his soul to him. In return the devil served him, and performed everything the doctor desired of him. But in the end, when his time had run out, the devil said: "Enough! Now, come!"

But Doctor Faust was not yet ready to go, and he

resisted as well as he could. He fought with curses and exorcisms, but in vain. The devil pounced on him and gripped him in his talons, and though Faust still resisted him, he burst out of the house with him, straight through the ceiling. And so Faust received what he had bargained for; he had sold himself to the devil, and the devil took him.

And the hole they made as they shot through the ceiling remained. It is true they tried to build over it several times, but every time the masonry had fallen out by morning, and there was the great black hole, just as before. At last they gave up trying, for they were frightened, especially when the spirit of Faust began to walk the house. Every night he haunted it, and soon not even the boldest tenant would remain in it.

From that time on no one moved in there, the ancient building stood empty. It decayed and mouldered steadily. No one so much as entered it, everyone preferred to avoid it and walk round its grounds, especially in the evening or night. But once in the autumn, when the day was already nearing twilight, a young student halted at the gate of Faust's house. That he was by no means well off was plain to be seen from his battered three-cornered hat, his worn-out coat and shiny knee-breeches, his darned stockings and down-at-heel shoes.

He was as poor as a stray greyhound. He had not even a roof over his head. He wandered through Prague, searching for lodgings, begging for a little time, but everywhere they refused him, and no one would take him in. So he had walked the whole day long, until weary and exhausted he stood before the house of Faust. He did not know himself how he had got there.

It was growing dark, a drizzling rain was falling and the wind blew bitterly cold. The student's shabby coat, though buttoned up to the neck, could not keep out the chill, and his miserable shoes let in the wet. He was already trembling with cold. The rain grew heavier, the night closed in; here he was in the autumnal evening, and where was he to spend the night?

He had nowhere to lay his head. He looked round him, and then fixed his eyes on the old and gloomy house. "They won't throw you out of here," he thought, and bitterness filled his heart. He hesitated for a moment, then he seized the latch; the door gave to his push, and he stood in a vaulted passage. It was dry, and no wind blew here. And since he had ventured so far, he mustered his courage and went on.

By a staircase, above which on his right hand curious statues stood in niches, he reached a corridor. It was long, and its distant end was lost in darkness. All along this corridor he saw a row of dark doors leading to various rooms. It was silent and deserted here within, but from the courtyard and the forsaken garden he heard the howling of the wind.

The young man considered for a while, and then

boldly reached for the latch of the nearest door and entered the room. Under its vaulted ceiling dusk was already gathering; the room seemed even more dim because the walls were covered to half their height with oak panelling, and all the furniture, the ancient table, cupboard and bench beside the wall, were of dark wood. Beside the table stood the dim shape of a high-backed armchair.

The student stood for a moment in the doorway, then he went in and sat down in the chair. He looked all round him, waiting and listening; but there was not a sound in the house, and no one appeared. Only the wind outside wailed, and the rain slashed and battered at the windows. The student in the armchair waited and listened, until weariness overwhelmed him, and the voices of rain and wind lulled him to sleep. He fell asleep, and slept until eleven, on past midnight, an hour after midnight; he slept until daybreak, and nothing disturbed him.

In the morning he awoke to wonder where he was, and when he remembered where he had passed the night, and how peacefully, he took heart. He did not take to his heels, but went curiously and even eagerly into the next room. It was furnished, and in addition there hung on the walls several faded and blackened pictures, in which he could distinguish little but the frowning faces of bearded men. But of the one-time owner of the house, Doctor Faust, of whom he was now thinking constantly, there was no trace.

Until he came to the third room. There stood an old bed, under a canopy of faded material, worn pillows lay on the ground, together with two overturned stools and an old tattered book in a yellowish binding which had once been white leather. And in the ceiling, a hole! It yawned blackly, as though torn out instantaneously and with great force.

The student halted at the sight of it. He remembered

what he had heard, and now he saw that everything in this room seemed to be just as it had been left when the devil carried off Doctor Faust. These stools he had over-turned, that book he had probably thrown at the devil. The young man did not venture to touch it, nor did he linger long in the room. In the next room he saw nothing odd, except that a flight of wooden stairs hung from the ceiling. He stepped onto the lowest stair and began to climb them, until he stood under the vaulted ceiling, where there was an opening through which he might go farther. As he stepped on the last stair he heard a rattle behind him, and looked round in alarm and wonder. The steps by which he had ascended had rolled themselves up as though made of paper, and vanished in the ceiling, above which he now stood in a new room, larger than all those through which he had passed. In his astonishment and excitement over his new discovery he forgot the stair-case and how he had come there.

The room was spacious, with a vaulted ceiling which bore pictures of the sun, stars and the heavenly bodies. Along the walls stood dark bookcases full of books in ancient bindings, small and large, and tables with various vessels of metal and glass, empty bottles and bottles full of tinctures coloured red, gold, blue and clear green. In the center of this great room stood a long table on crossed legs, covered with a green cloth, and on it gleamed vessels of brass and copper, a variety of measuring instruments and gauges, and beside these a number of yellowed parchments and papers, some blank, some written on. There was also an open book beneath a pewter candlestick holding a wax candle, burned well down. Everything appeared as though someone had only recently left the room.

In this apartment the student lingered longest. When he returned to the opening by which he had entered it, and stepped upon the threshold, the wooden stairs unfolded and descended again of their own accord to the floor below, so that he was free to go down whenever he pleased. From the lower room he did not enter Faust's bedroom again, but let himself out by another door into the entrance hall. There he saw a statue of a slender boy with a drum slung round him by a strap. As the young man approached him and touched the drum, the boy started as though he had been alive, and began to drum. The drumsticks fairly flashed, and the drum rolled until it was a wonder the window didn't rattle. The boy drummed and drummed, and the student in a fright ran out into the corridor.

Thence he hurried into the open passage, and so to the deserted courtyard, where on the edge of the garden there was a well. Yellow lichen and green moss had overgrown its sandstone ashlars, and the fallen leaves of maples and limes, gold and red, were strewn over the water and the chipped stone statue of a strange monster.

He explored the garden, too, but there he did not linger long.

Under the old trees, among the briars and undergrowth on a murky autumn day, it was not cheerful. He returned into the house. It was silent there now; the boy had stopped drumming. The young man did not go near him, but returned by the staircase into the great vaulted room and examined the parchments and papers scattered there. Beneath them he found a smooth, glistening dish of black marble, and in it a silver coin, bright and gleaming like new.

He was delighted but also frightened. For a while he stood over it considering what to do with it. He had not a farthing in his pockets, and he was beginning to be hungry. But what if Faust, or the devil himself——?

He hesitated, he dreaded, but in the end he took the coin and went off into the town. In the evening he returned, having eaten his fill, but with the haunting fear that some spirit might appear in the night. He sat down in the chair, as on the previous night, to sleep away the hours of darkness. He did not fall asleep so readily as before, and he awoke during the night. But neither the spirit of Faust nor the devil appeared to him.

When he again examined the library and the instruments on the table, once again there was a silver coin lying in the black marble dish. Yesterday there had been one also, just one, and he had taken it and changed it in the town; he had some small change from it still in his pockets. And now, in the same place from which he had taken it, there it was again, a coin gleaming white as milk against the black dish. This was surely meant for him. Doctor Faust or somebody had sent it to him. So the student reasoned, and he took the coin.

Before noon he left the house, and returned again in the evening, bringing the remains of the second coin in his pockets. And again he slept in the house, and as peacefully as before. The next morning on rising he went straight to the library and looked on the table. And there it was, a coin as pure as though fresh from the mint, lying on the black dish. The young man no longer doubted that it was for him, and took it without hesitation.

And so every morning he found a coin there. He did not need so much for his daily expenses. He saved up the change until he had enough to buy new clothes, a cloak, a hat and new shoes. He was doing very well for himself. He did not bother about finding lodgings now; he was no longer afraid in the house of Faust, he had grown accustomed to his silent dwelling, where some spirit took care of his needs, and yet never showed himself. In winter he had plenty of wood there, both in the courtyard and the garden. He laid fires and lit them to warm his house, until the flames burned and crackled pleasantly downstairs in the stove, or up in the library in the hearth. He read and read in the books from Faust's library, and also in the book he had found on the large table, and the one below in the bedroom. It was a long time before he ventured to touch that one, but it was there in particular that he found what interested him, for it was full of strange signs and incantations. With dread he began to read, and sometimes his hair stood on end as he studied these sorceries.

Sometimes, too, his solitude oppressed him, but he did not want to move. He had peace here, and was comfortable enough, and moreover he had a coin a day without working for it! His companions at the college, where he put in an appearance less and less frequently, wondered what had happened to him and what was still happening to change him so, and make such a dandy of him. They froze in consternation when they heard where he was living, and were reluctant to visit him when he invited them. At last curiosity drew some of them to the house. He led them all through it, from the passage to the upper floor, through entrance hall, rooms, library; he showed them the bedroom, with the bed newly furnished, for now he himself slept in it. The hole in the ceiling was covered and blocked up with a carpet. He took them through the garden, and showed them everything that he himself had discovered during his stay in the old building.

They talked with amazement of the wonders of this secret dwelling, of the boy who drummed of his own accord, of strange statues that sang softly, of the metal maiden who poured water for them, of the miraculous latch on the door of one of the rooms, that shot out sparks and wounded whoever touched it, of the room into which a flight of steps let itself down from the ceiling, and again rolled itself up into the ceiling, of the strange instruments and magical books. He even told them about the iron door that led down into an underground chamber beneath the house, and thence to a long, dark passage.

The only thing about which the student did not boast to his friends was the black dish and its silver coins. But he laughed at his friends when they warned him not to stay in the house; all this was merely temporary, they said, suddenly something would happen to him, some evil spirit would ambush him.

They were not talking nonsense. The charm of the black dish was a trap set for him.

He had a coin every day, there was no need for him to worry about anything or do anything. He grew accustomed to comfort and ease, and began to have more lavish fancies, to dress expensively and treat himself to luxuries; his expenses mounted, but the amount in the dish remained the same. A silver coin a day was no longer enough.

The student had got out of the habit of living modestly. He had forgotten what his state had been when he came here. And now he could not face the thought of working. He fell back upon his books, the one from the table in the great library, and the one he had picked up in the bedroom. In them he had read how to conjure, and how to call up spirits. They themselves had so far never revealed themselves to him, he had been at peace from them; and he himself, until this moment, had not summoned them. He was afraid, and still hesitated. But now the desire for gold urged and compelled him. Silver was no longer enough for him. Not even a dish full of silver coins would have sufficed; he wanted gold, and these books must help him to gain it.

One day he spent the entire day revelling in Prague, and frittered away borrowed money. During this revel he boastfully urged his boon companions and hangers-on to drink deeply and not spare the expense, for tomorrow he would have even more money. Gold, nothing but gold, and not borrowed, but his own; for he would force the spirit who had served him thus far to provide him with gold ducats instead of modest silver coins.

Late in the evening he left them to return to the house of Faust. Several of his drunken companions wished to go with him, but he would not allow them. Today he must be alone, he said, for tonight he would have important work. They gazed after him as he went in, and the wicket in the heavy gate closed after him. They never saw him again; neither they nor any other living soul. He never appeared again in the college, nor anywhere else.

When several of his friends who had already visited the house with him went to look for him there, they could not find him. Within the house it was hushed, silent, deserted, not a sign of the student anywhere. But in the bedroom they found the bed in disorder, the pillows on the floor, clothes scattered, a cloak torn to shreds, chairs overturned, and on the paving a battered old book of magic, an overturned candlestick and a burned-out candle.

Everything showed that someone had been involved in a struggle here. The carpet lay discarded on the ground, torn to pieces, and the black hole gaped wide. Round its edges they saw on the ceiling stains, as though blood had spilled there. And not dark blood, but fresh, spilled not long ago.

All the students crossed themselves and fled in terror from the house of Faust. They were overwhelmed with horror at the terrible end that had overtaken their comrade. He had surely called up an evil spirit, summoned him proudly, and the evil spirit had settled accounts with him. He had vanished with him through the hole in the ceiling, through which long ago he had flown with Doctor Faust.

Ingeborg Bachmann

BOHEMIA

IF BOHEMIA STILL lies by the sea, I'll believe. in the
sea.
And if I believe in the sea, I can hope for land.

If I'm the one, then anyone is, he's worth as much as I.
I want nothing more for myself. Let me go under now.

---

*Austrian writer Ingeborg Bachmann is recognized as a major influence on
modern German writers Günter Grass, Christa Wolf, and Peter Handke.
Her collections of poetry won her the Georg Büchner prize in 1964.
"Bohemia" was written in the mid-1940s.*

Go under—that means to the ocean, there I'll find
Bohemia again.
From my ruins, I wake up in peace.
From deep down I know, and am not lost.

Come here, all you Bohemians, seamen, harbor whores
and ships
unanchored. Don't you want to be Bohemians, all you
Illyrians,
Venetians and Veronese. Play the comedies that make us
laugh

to our tears. And go astray a hundred times,
as I went astray and never stood the trials.
Yet I did stand them, each and every time.

As Bohemia stood them and one fine day
was pardoned to the sea and now lies by water.

I still border on a word and a different land,
I border, like little else, on everything more and more,

a man from Bohemia, a vagrant, a player
who has nothing and whom nothing holds,
granted only, by a questionable sea, to gaze at the land of
my choice.

J o s e f   S k v o r e c k y

PIRATES

THE FATAL WOUND was unusual. "A blow from the left side," said Dr. Seifert, "probably by a blunt object; but I can't quite figure it out. It doesn't look like the object was hard. A rubber truncheon, maybe, but the mark seems too narrow for that. It's strange."

The corpse was strange as well. It lay, still warm, in the dark stairwell of an eighteenth-century tenement house

Josef Skvorecky is a novelist, essayist, critic, and filmmaker. In the 1960s, his stories and alternative films made him a Czech folk hero. "Pirates" is from his collection of detective tales, The End of Lieutenant Boruvka *(1990).*

in Mala Strana. Sergeant Pudil was leaning keenly over it, examining the head, which was cocked at an unnatural angle against the right shoulder. Lieutenant Boruvka suddenly realized that he felt nothing at all towards the murdered old man, and he was ashamed at his own callousness. There had been a time, not so long ago, when each murder victim seemed like a tragically unfinished novel. But the old man with the broken neck awakened other sensations in him; it was as though someone, in a fit of rage, had tried to destroy evidence of his political past.

The sergeant looked up from the corpse. "I'll be hanged if it isn't karate, comrade. They showed us exactly the same kind of bruises in the course."

THIS SENTENCE WAS still ringing in the lieutenant's ears as the superintendent opened the door to the dead man's flat. The sergeant looked around like an animal sniffing the wind. The apartment consisted of a kitchen and one room which was dominated by a large certificate in a frame, the kind that used to enclose portraits of aristocratic ladies.

THE PRAGUE COMMITTEE OF THE UNION OF CZECHOSLOVAK-SOVIET FRIENDSHIP TAKES GREAT PLEASURE IN NAMING FRANTISEK NOVOTNY AN HONORARY MEMBER ON THE OCCASION OF HIS SEVENTY-FIFTH BIRTHDAY

There were no other certificates on the walls. The document seemed rather slender recognition for a lifetime of dedication, the lieutenant reflected. What had the dead man been?

"He worked in an office at the Ministry of Heavy Industry," the superintendent told them. "But he's been retired for fifteen years. He worked for another eight or so, then it got too much for him and he packed it in."

The sergeant lifted a strange object from the table and held it up in the light streaming into the room through a dirty window. The object glistened. It was a bronzed bust made of papier-mâché, a kind he had not seen—at least not in public—for a long time. The sergeant stared respectfully at the lackluster bust of Stalin. Then, along with the lieutenant, he looked at the wall opposite the framed certificate. On it hung a portrait of the late Klement Gottwald, the man officially known as the first working-class president, who had died of "Moscow flu" just days after the demise of his mentor, Josef Stalin.

Above a writing table there was yet another devotional portrait from the official pantheon: a photograph, to which a black band of mourning had been affixed across the lower left-hand corner. The lieutenant didn't know who the man in the photograph was, and was just about to ask the superintendent when he heard Malek behind him saying, "Josef! Take a gander at this!"

The lieutenant turned around. Malek was holding something even more unusual than the bust of Stalin, something vaguely resembling an army radio receiver with two sets of wires running out of it, one ending in earphones, the other in a flat, circular object with a rubber ring around it. It was this that Malek was holding out for the lieutenant.

But the sergeant got there first. Eagerly he grasped the earphones and shot a glance at Malek, who quickly handed him the whole device. The sergeant, though obviously unfamiliar with this technology, was as usual undeterred by his own ignorance. Frowning, he put the flat round rubber object to his eye and peered inside. The old detective let him examine the rubbery darkness for a while before remarking, "It's a listening device. There's a special microphone inside the plate that can pick up a conversation through a three-foot wall. That rubber rim is a suction device for attaching . . ."

"Well, I'll be!" whistled the sergeant. "So he was a . . .

and the karate . . . Comrades! It all fits together! The karate! Do you see?"

The only response from the others was silence. The lieutenant donned his sphinxlike expression—something he did rather frequently these days, though it looked more like an uncomprehending moon. Malek wore the look of a retarded country bumpkin and Dr. Seifert's face was the mask of a man whose expertise is in a different field altogether.

"Look, you've got the karate, you've got this counter-espionage device, you've got the former employee of a vital ministry, you put it all together and . . ."

He looked around and saw a shadow of suspicion cross the lieutenant's neutral mask.

"All right. I know. I was a little too hasty about that Zionist. And I admitted it, too, in the spirit of self-criticism. But then there was no listening device, no karate, just a hammer. . . ."

The sergeant hesitated. He had made many overly hasty judgments in almost two years of service with Lieutenant Boruvka and each time he had owned up. Once he had even inflicted a minor gunshot wound on a man he was arresting—inappropriately rather than mistakenly, as it later turned out—for murder. When the man had reached into his breast pocket in the familiar gesture of one about to display his badge, the sergeant, who had a secret passion for the American westerns that had recently flooded the cinemas to replace Vera Chytilova's formalistic films, interpreted the man's movement *à la* OK Corral. He got his shot away—or so he thought—as quickly as the Sundance Kid, but fortunately not as accurately, so that ultimately the sister security organization was not deprived of a rather important hitman. Sergeant Pudil was reprimanded but allowed to remain in the lieutenant's group, despite the old detective's suggestion that he be transferred to Petty Theft. The incident had badly shaken the sergeant's self-confidence, but instead of knuckling under, he intensified his efforts, driven by the hope of one day capturing James Bond—whom the sergeant, having been misled by references to Bond in the leading Party newspaper, believed to be a real person, a colleague from the far shore.

Now the lieutenant had taken him somewhat aback, and he was worried about having to submit to another round of self-criticism. But he restored his confidence by examining the certificate in the gold frame, then the deceased president, and finally the generalissimo's bust. As his conviction grew, he took the special microphone by the cord and, swinging it round like a slingshot, looked at the photograph with the mourning band. Lieutenant Boruvka, Malek, Dr. Seifert, and the superintendent followed the journey of his eyes until the superintendent could hold back no longer.

"That's Comrade Jidas," he said. "They were friends.

Comrade Jidas was one of that group that invited in the Soviets. . . ."

"That clinches it," said Sergeant Pudil, this time with utter conviction.

IN THE NEXT flat on the left lived a couple called the Blazeks, but they only interested the sergeant for a moment. As soon as the superintendent told him who lived in the flat on the right, all his most intrinsic abilities were aroused. He put the earphones on and began listening through the wall.

"There's a bunch of people in there and they're all talking at once," he reported. "And it's anti-state talk."

"Is that a fact?" said the lieutenant with insincere surprise. "In that case, I'd better look into it alone. They won't feel they have to pretend in front of me. I . . . ," he explained hastily, "I happen to know Kopanec. His niece used to work with me before she got married.

Kopanec trusts me completely. I'll just sort of drop in—
by chance. We mustn't arouse their suspicions. . . ."

"The bastards!" exploded the sergeant. "They're
insulting our first working-class pres . . ."

"Off I go," said the lieutenant quickly. "I'll take care of
it myself. You go back to headquarters and . . . and . . . "
He could hardly get it past his lips, for a sudden terror
came over him—a terror that came from a longing to help
where he had no business doing so, at least, not as a member of the Public Security force. But there was that old
record in his daughter's room, played so often during the
past two years that he could scarcely understand the words
any more. "And phone the comrades at Interior. Ask them
to send you material on Novotny . . . and on the Blazeks
too, of course. And everyone in the building. The comrade
here will give you a list. . . ."

He nodded towards the superintendent, but the
sergeant said, "We're going in there with you, comrade!"

It sounded almost like a threat. A wave of red anger swept through the old detective and he roared back at his subordinate, "You're going to phone Interior. And that's an order. And I'm a first lieutenant, in case you've forgotten, comrade sergeant!"

The two years Pudil had spent in the company of his mild-mannered superior officer had not prepared him for such an outburst. But the Pavlovian reflex worked and he blurted, "Yes, sir, comrade first lieutenant!"

"WELL, I DO declare!" said the writer through the half-open door. Somewhere above him, the doorbell was tinkling a phrase from "Ach, du lieber Augustin." As usual, the writer was mildly tipsy. "You haven't come to put the cuffs on me again, have you, lieutenant? Last time you didn't get very far, but now I'd like to confess up front, without the torture, if you don't mind. I have a very low threshold of pain."

"Can I talk to you alone, Master?" whispered the lieutenant.

Kopanec chuckled. "Won't be 'master' for quite a while yet. I'm still a mere tyro. Digging the new subway. There are no master craftsmen in that field . . . just laborers."

"It's about a serious matter. Can we discuss it alone for a bit?"

Kopanec looked around. A company of intoxicated men and women was sitting in the room on the floor, the coffee table, and the sideboard were strewn with bottles, some opened, some still corked. Except for a dim light cast by some candles and, in the corner, a dark red Chinese lantern bearing the portrait of Mao Tse Tung, the room was almost dark.

"*The Lonely Crowd*," intoned Kopanec. "And here we are in that crowd, alone. That's the safest way in these times, lieutenant."

"Shh!" said the lieutenant in alarm. "Call me . . . call me Novak, let's say," he whispered. "It's a delicate business. I don't want . . ."

Kopanec turned towards the room and announced ceremoniously, "Comrades, I'd like you to meet a rare and precious guest. Mr. Novak. A former physical education teacher. At present without permanent employment. An old and trusted friend of mine, so you can carry on talking to your heart's content."

Several people raised their wine glasses and a man whose face was vaguely familiar to the lieutenant resumed talking, probably where he had left off when he had been interrupted by the lieutenant's knock.

"I treat it like a traffic accident. It's a shock at first, but sooner or later you have to get over it. I say you only have the moral right to leave the country if your life's in actual danger."

"By the time you find that out, it's always too late,

isn't it?" said a woman. She didn't look old, but her hair was prematurely gray.

"Those days are over, Sarka," said the speaker earnestly. "Today even *they* know you can't undo a knot with a sword. . . ."

"When you've got a chronic kidney problem like me," said a bald-headed man, "two years in the cooler can knock twenty years off your life."

"You should worry," said the woman called Sarka. "Keep on hitting the booze like that and your chronic kidneys won't last two years. In the sunshine."

The lieutenant listened, fascinated. Kopanec took him by the arm. "Leave them be. As usual, they're trying to square the circle. In my opinion, it's a bloody mess no matter what you call it—car accident or cultural genocide. I'm an expert on bloody messes. And I say we're all buried in shit right up to here—Prague, San Francisco, it doesn't matter a damn."

He led the lieutenant to a dark corner where two armchairs sat buried under stacks of yellowed magazines. The writer carefully lifted the magazines and put them down on the carpet. The lieutenant saw that they were old copies of something called *The Occult Review*.

"I've taken up science," Kopanec explained. "Nowadays the daily press specializes in pure mysticism, so I thought, what the hell, and borrowed these from my great-grand-mother. You didn't happen to know my great-grandfather, by any chance? Ran a clairvoyance lab in Nerudova Street. Those were the days, by God," he sighed, pouring the lieutenant and himself a drink from a bottle that was only available in the foreign-currency shops. "Great-grandad was in the slammer during the war. The Nazis shut down scientific operations like his, as you know, but he kept at it on the sly. He was a cautious old bugger, but his destiny caught up with him in the end. Ah, well." He sighed, and they touched glasses.

"Did he survive the war? asked the lieutenant considerately. The expert in bloody messes appeared not to have heard the question.

"Once they stuck an informer in with him. Grandad knew the guy was a stool pigeon, so he told his fortune, predicted he'd get to be an *Oberscharführer* in the Saint Wenceslas SS division. A bad psychological mistake that was, because by that time the war was in its dying days and a career in the SS was the furthest thing from the fink's mind. What he wanted to know was whether he was going to keep his neck out of a noose after the war, and he was pissed off because he thought Grandad was having some fun at his expense. But anyway, he survived."

"Who, your great-grandad?" asked the lieutenant, while trying to think of the most considerate—and tactful—way to inform the writer that the noose, or at least arrest, was now threatening *him*.

"You kidding? He wouldn't lay off, read the screws' palms in prison and they hanged him for it. It was the informer who survived. Never got to be an *Oberscharführer,* but I hear he's not so badly off. I have an idea," and he squinted with malicious delight at the lieutenant, "that he's even a colleague of yours. At least, that's my impression. He's titular head of some department in the Historical Institute, but, I mean . . ."

The lieutenant gave his standard, automatic response: "I'm with the *criminal* police. That's why I'm here."

"Oh, dearie me! Don't tell me another girl's in trouble? But the girls don't swarm around me the way they used to, lieutenant. Not since I've been swinging a pick for a living. I don't mean to suggest they discriminate on the basis of class, not at all. But you know how it is, I just haven't got the personal charm of a man like Vrchcolab." And the master of bloody messes glanced enviously at the man holding court in the living room.

"They won't do you the pleasure," the bald man was just saying to him. "You've got too high a profile. There's no percentage in making world-famous martyrs any more. Even they know that by now."

The lieutenant shuddered. He remembered where he knew Vrchcolab from: he was always being attacked in the papers. Boruvka admired the man's courage. Once again, he felt those man-eating fish from the Paraná River nipping away at his conscience.

"That's precisely why I do what I do. The world must be told what's going on here."

"What world do you mean?" asked the bald man. "The one that lounges about by the swimming pool with a newspaper in one hand and a mint julep in the other? What other world is there?"

The lieutenant listened again, fascinated. "So tell me about it," he heard Kopanec's voice say. "Another ballerina? Otherwise I'm not interested."

With great effort, the old detective turned his attention from his private thoughts back to objective reality and said, "It's your neighbor. He's been murdered. And . . . ," he lowered his whisper until it was scarcely audible, "I have reason to suspect—in fact I'm practically certain—that he worked for . . . the organization I *don't* belong to. There was a bugging device in his flat. He was probably listening to what you were saying here when . . ."

"No matter," said the writer calmly. "There's already a microphone over there in the radiator and another one in the telephone."

The lieutenant was visibly shaken and the writer slapped himself on the forehead. "Oh Christ!" He lowered his voice to a whisper even less audible than the lieutenant's. "A thousand pardons. I guess they haven't got you on tape yet, have they? God the last thing I want to do is get you in trouble. . . ."

He got up, took the phone off the hook, and tossed a thick blanket over the radiator. The lieutenant's knees began to tremble. "Normally we don't bother any more, because they can hardly find out anything about us they don't already know." He looked around at the company and so did the lieutenant. Once again, his attention was drawn to Vrchcolab.

"It doesn't matter if not a soul *over there* takes any notice," he was saying. "The important thing is that it be said *here!*"

"To guarantee yourself a place in history, right?" said the bald man sarcastically.

"So it won't vanish from history altogether," Vrchcolab shot back.

The lieutenant was ashamed that he couldn't control the trembling of his own limbs. He wasn't a coward. He had proven this again and again in situations that were a matter of life and death, not just of prison. But now he was afraid.

On those occasions he had always stood alone with a pistol, facing someone who was also alone with a pistol. The odds were even. Now he was afraid. Kopanec whispered into his ear, "I'd feel awful if you were to get in trouble over this. I know you're a good man. My niece Eva told me a lot about you. There was once a time, if I'm not mistaken, when she was nuts over you. But I don't suppose you're interested in such things. You're a lucky man. Eva's already had two kids with that brain surgeon of hers, did you know?"

The lieutenant was afraid. At the mention of the progeny of the former policewoman with the magnificent chignon, he realized that it was not for himself that he was afraid. *People can be brought to heel if they are afraid and have a lot of children. . . .* In his mind he heard the voice of the sweat-soaked writer, and he began to tremble. "Really? I'm glad to hear it," he said sincerely, though somewhat absently. "And I . . . I was fond of your niece, too, I won't deny it. But she . . ."

"Maybe you didn't say anything improper," the writer interrupted him, once again speaking in that microphonophobic whisper. "Or did you? What did you say, anyway?"

"Nothing. Unless. . . ," and the lieutenant adjusted his whisper to match Kopanec's, "as I told you, the murdered man worked for the Ministry of the Interior. . . ."

"You said that in a whisper. I know for a fact that the mike won't pick up whispers when others are speaking out loud in the same room, like now. What a racket!"

"You're no better than a collaborator!" someone was shouting. "You act in those shit-bag plays of theirs while others can't even get a foot in the door any more!"

"Isn't he wonderful? You'd be delighted to act in those shit-bag plays if only they'd let you, darling!"

The lieutenant had to agree that a conversation of such intensity must have drowned out his incriminating remark.

"Who do you think did him in?" whispered Kopanec.

The old detective shrugged his shoulders and asked, "No one left here in the last hour or so?"

"No. This bunch has been here since six."

"Not even briefly?"

"I'm sure of it. The john's inside here, not on the balcony, and I've got those chimes on the main entrance. Kind of a joke. I bought them in Vienna once. Those were the days, I tell you. *Ach, du lieber Augustin!*" he recited dreamily, then suddenly spat out, "*Alles ist hin!*" He shook his head resolutely. "I'd have noticed if anyone left. That song is becoming a royal pain in the ass, I should disconnect the goddamn thing." He looked at the lieutenant. "What is it? Did you think of something?"

The lieutenant had fallen into a trancelike state that signaled profound thought. As if in a dream, he asked, "Are you absolutely sure your flat is bugged?"

"Want to bet it isn't? But I can't take bets on that, it wouldn't be fair. Of course it's bugged." He was still whispering. "Once—about a year after the fraternal assistance brigades rode their tanks into town—the cops called me in for some friendly little interrogations. Went on for about a month, and they'd play me tapes with scenes from my older domestic performances, even before the invasion. Some of them involved a certain young lady. They were okay, only mildly anti-state and only occasionally. But once they played me a monologue—I had no idea myself I'd ever uttered anything so enlightened. Of course, I was looped at the time, which, as we know is not an extenuating circumstance in our scientifically established state— and rightly so. I still don't know why they didn't throw the book at me."

"I don't understand it," said the lieutenant.

"Neither do I," said Kopanec. "When Tony Novotny was president—may the good Lord grant him eternal glory—I would have got a year, probably more."

"That's not what I mean. There's something else I don't understand."

"I don't understand any of it," said Kopanec, taking a drink. "I don't understand a goddamn thing any more, my dear lieutenant."

"God, how our holy émigrés carry on!" another voice was shouting. "They leave the country, they live like pigs in clover, and instead of turning their backs and saying 'good riddance!' they can't stop writing about us. The bastards probably make their living at it, so they make damn good and sure the interest doesn't dry up on them."

"You sound like an editorial in *Tribuna*," said Sarka.

"Occasionally something with a grain of truth in it gets into *Tribuna* by mistake," the drunken voice went on. "The sooner the emigrants shit on us and get off the pot, the sooner the Commies will lay off and let us get on with it."

"Get on with shit," said the bald man. "Not that I have anything against shit. But during the so-called years of deformation, your line was 'complete freedom or nothing,' because without absolute freedom, you can only do what's permitted. You even let them quote you in the Western press, and that was at a time when I was saying privately that it's better to have what's permitted than nothing at all. Well, now you've got your nothing; so what the fuck are you complaining about?"

"I don't hold it against anyone for leaving," said another voice. "I can understand that. Some people were afraid nothing could be done. . . ."

"They were afraid they'd end up in Siberia, the heroes," shouted another drunken voice. "Now they're all cozy and safe and they've got courage to burn. At home, while we were trying to get things moving, they collaborated!"

"You tried so hard to get things moving they gave you a state prize," said the bald man, "while they were hounding me for existentialism."

"No, no, there's something else," the lieutenant was whispering. "Perhaps you can help me."

"Me? I can't even help myself," said the famous writer sadly.

"Look, he was working for . . . for *them.* He must have known you had a permanent bug in your flat, so it's not logical that he would have listened to you with a portable device."

The writer gave him a dumb look. "Maybe he was just eager."

"Maybe," said the lieutenant. "But who are those people living on the other side?"

"Someone called Blazek and his wife. Pensioners."

"Pensioners?" The lieutenant thought for a moment. The murdered man had been a pensioner too, his head oddly bent towards his right shoulder. Karate? Perhaps What sort of person would be likely to know karate in this country? "How old are they?"

"Don't know, exactly, but over seventy for sure."

"What kind of shape are they in, physically?"

"The old geezer has asthma. Takes him about an hour to walk up to the third floor. That's in summer. Takes him twice as long in winter. His wife seems a little more chipper, but she's got rheumatism in her lower back or something. She looks like she's been gathering mushrooms all her life. She walks bent over at right angles."

Karate! But why was he listening in on them? They don't hand out bugging devices just to find out if two old people tottering on the brink of the grave are fulsome enough in their praise of the first secretary.

"They do *not* live like pigs in clover over there," said a woman's voice, one the lieutenant had not yet heard. "They have to work hard for what they get. My husband, for example, works every other weekend. . . ."

"What did you marry him for then, if he's such a poor, exploited wretch? And anyway, he's a Kraut," said a stout young man.

"I'm not complaining," the girl shot back. "I just mentioned him to demonstrate that your eyes are bigger than your brains. Things aren't all that great in the West either, you know."

"Hey, hey, none of that, now!" said another voice. "You've turned into an agent of socialism over there, Jaruska. Go on back to Paris, where it's still fashionable to talk like that."

"Oh God, you're all being so impossible!" said the girl. "I'm good for sending you ten LPs a month, aren't I? You have any idea how much they cost? And new dresses from Printemps for your darling Bohuna so the poor dear won't suffer. And even so, she badmouths me. She tells all her friends I buy them at the fleamarket because she thinks only Schiaparellis are good enough for her."

"And don't you buy clothes at the fleamarket?" said another girl cattily.

"Yes, I do. But only for myself. That's all I have money left for."

"So why do you send things here, darling?"

"So you won't badmouth me, darling. But you do anyway, I know it. People from Prague write me everything, and the censors let gossip through. In Paris we know everything that goes on."

"You know sweet nothing there!"

"You know sweet nothing *here!*"

The lieutenant, drawn to the conversation against his will once more, shook his round head and asked, "Do the Blazeks have a boarder or anything like that?"

"No, only a granddaughter."

"How old?"

"About six, I think. Her name is Jana. She'll be going to school in the fall."

"An orphan?"

Kopanec grinned wryly. "A state orphan, you might say. I don't know what the official terminology for it is. Her parents quote betrayed their country unquote by escaping when the fraternal assistance brigade arrived. They thought—naively—that there were some international agreements about reuniting families. And who am I to say? Maybe there are. All I know is that the only ones that exist and are adhered to are agreements about shipments of wheat, and maybe pipeline components. There's nothing about the shipment of children. There's no profit in children."

He realized that the lieutenant was not listening.

"I happen to know also," shrilled the girl who had married the Parisian Kraut, "that your old man is sucking up to that whore Balabasova, so they'll at least let him translate some half-assed Russian play under someone else's name!"

"And I happen to know," said the other girl even

more shrilly, "that you're two-timing that capitalist husband of yours with your former lover who's now working for Radio Free Europe. And I'll write him about it, you'd better believe it. That much French I do know!"

The lieutenant, though he was thinking about something else, was still astonished at the efficiency of modern communications and at the powerlessness of all the mechanisms and measures designed to eliminate private interests in the name of the state. He came to his feet like a sleepwalker.

"Are you all right?" asked Kopanec, concerned. "Why, you haven't even touched a drop."

The old detective only shook his head. To the tune of the song about dear Augustin, he went out into the hallway.

"DO YOU KNOW Jana Blazek?" he said to a boy in a young pioneer's kerchief, who stood by the courtyard pump playing with a yo-yo that displayed a garish portrait of Mickey Mouse.

"Yup."

"Look," said the lieutenant, "I'll give you ten crowns if you'll go to the Blazeks' and ask Jana to come out and play with you."

"Make it Tuzex crowns," said the boy.

The old detective sighed, reached into his pocket, and pulled out a scruffy wallet bearing a picture of the New York skyline. It contained five banknotes of the desired kind, which had been sent to his daughter from Memphis. He intended to use them in the foreign-currency shop to buy a product called Instant Cocoa for his granddaughter. He gave one to the boy and stuck the wallet, a gift from his son-in-law, back into his pocket.

"One more," said the young pioneer.

Out came the wallet with the picture of New York on

it and the little boy got what he asked for. He rolled the bill up, stuck the Mickey Mouse yo-yo into his pocket, and said, "The Blazeks won't let her come out, because it's too late. But I'll try anyway, so you can't say I didn't."

He ran upstairs through the dark corridor.

The lieutenant leaned against the pump and looked at the buildings facing the courtyard. Old baroque houses, once witness to the small, inconsequential human tragedies captured so well by the writer Jan Neruda. The lieutenant had not read Neruda's *Mala Strana Tales* for a long time—not, in fact, since he'd been a student at the Kostelec grammar school. But Neruda's name often came up during political schooling sessions. Jan Neruda had also written an essay on the First of May, and Boruvka's instructors had told him that he was, in fact, a socialist agent. No, they hadn't called him an agent, he corrected himself; that was what someone had called the girl who had married a German

Parisian. The writer had merely been a socialist. That was where the difference lay. Perhaps.

He could hear the sound of a phonograph coming from an open window somewhere. His daughter, Zuzana, had the same song in her well-played record collection. She was no longer the same Zuzana who had once, long ago, secretly telephoned Olda Spacek because she couldn't solve an ordinary equation with a single unknown. She was now a mother—and a wife.

Leaning against the pump, the lieutenant could not stop the flow of memories. They were all recent. They had to do with waiting in corridors, spelled off by Mrs. Boruvka, filling out requests, waiting in the outer offices of people he believed could do something. The boy with the yo-yo reminded him of his vain attempt to bribe a bigwig who promised to help and then reneged with the excuse that there was nothing he could do, which might well have been true. In any case, he didn't return the money. That had been Tuzex currency too, also from Memphis, Tennessee. "Help me, Information," said the lieutenant to himself, for though the record was so worn it was scarcely comprehensible, and though his knowledge of English was scanty, the words had burned themselves into his memory like a magic spell, like a prayer, like a formula of longing, of meager hope and enormous despair. The distant phonograph on the fourth floor was now playing another sad song:

No matter what the future brings
I love you more than anything

The lieutenant wiped a tear away with the wide palm of his hand, and fumbled for his handkerchief.

The boy ran out of the dark corridor, his Mickey Mouse yo-yo once again readied for action.

"Jana's not home," he announced.

"And where is she?"

"She went to visit her aunt in Mydloves."

The lieutenant said nothing. He knew the village. It was in the south, close to the West German border. He stared blankly at nothing, unperceiving. The distant phonograph on the fourth floor played on.

> They told me on the way, they
> told me, "Joe
> There's no way she'll be yours again
> no more. . . ."

The boy with the Mickey Mouse yo-yo stared at him in alarm. There were tears streaming down the old man's cheeks. He was still staring at him when the man stumbled through the courtyard gate into the street, where the first gas lamps were just being lit.

BACK AT THE department, an excited pair was waiting for him. "There's a suspicious bunch at Kopanec's place," he said. "Full of people connected with the Dubcek era."

"Wrong, comrade lieutenant!" Pudil didn't even let him finish. "I don't mean to say you're not right. But this time it wasn't any of them. You'll flip when I tell you what Comrade Malek and I found out at Interior."

The lieutenant abandoned his effort to lead the exemplary young security agent off the track.

"Ever heard the name Joe Bomb?" asked Pudil.

The old detective shook his head.

"I'll bet you haven't. He's a very careful bird, this one. A Czech-American. Left in 1939 when the Nazis came. You get me?"

Despite the weariness he felt come over him, the lieutenant managed a wry smile. "He's a Zionist, you mean."

This surprised the sergeant. "I—jeez, I forgot to check on that. But never mind. There's no time for that now. His name used to be Bambasek, but in the U.S.A. he changed it to Bomb. Anyway, this fellow Bomb has come into the country twice in the last month. Twice! In one month!"

"Kopanec had a loud argument yesterday with Novotny," said the lieutenant weakly. "The whole house heard it."

"Not surprising," said the sergeant, "but irrelevant in this connection. On his first visit, this Joe Bomb fellow dropped in on two people. And now, hang on to your socks!"

The lieutenant had no need to brace himself. He could sense what was coming.

"The first was a woman called Cermak in a place called Mydloves. It's in the Sumava foothills."

"Why?" asked the lieutenant without interest.

"Just hang on. The second visit is really interesting. Blazek!! Novotny's next-door neighbor! And you know why?"

"No," said the lieutenant. "Are they related?"

"That's just it. They're not. But Bomb lives in Pittsburgh. And the Blazeks have a daughter who skipped the country with her husband after the fraternal troops intervened, and they ended up in Pittsburgh!"

"First we thought he was just bringing some family messages," said Malek uneasily. "But the whole thing's a lot more complicated."

The sergeant then began to tell the old detective a story he himself had already partly pieced together while waiting by the pump in the baroque courtyard. The man who had changed his name to Joe Bomb was not related to Mrs. Cermak of Mydloves. But Mrs. Cermak was another daughter of the pensioners who were Novotny's neighbors.

"His first trip here wasn't so suspicious," said Pudil. "But the second one! He arrived three days ago and the first person he meets isn't a relative of his either. Someone called Oldrich Spacek, an aviation engineer who works for Avia. And there's a connection here too that's got nothing to do with family."

The lieutenant felt the shock of sudden panic. He knew the engineer from Avia better than he cared to admit. He became terribly afraid lest Zuzana, whom Oldrich Spacek had once helped out in mathematics and God knows what else, might somehow be dragged into this affair as well.

"Spacek," the sergeant went on, "is a pilot in the Army Aeronautics Club, Svazarm. And Svazarm," he said, grinning, "has an airfield in Mydloves!"

He paused to see what the old detective would say but, when he said nothing, Pudil went on: "I don't suppose it makes any sense to you, does it? Well, I'm not surprised. Because there's a missing link. And that link is called Jana Blazek. She's six years old and she's the daughter of those escapees in Pittsburgh."

"Oh, so that's it," sighed the lieutenant.

"They want to kidnap her, the pirates!" the sergeant shouted. "But they've counted their chickens too soon. Public Security in Mydloves has already been given the alarm. They'll let us know the minute Joe Bomb shows up there with the girl!" He calmed down somewhat and added, "Oh, I almost forgot to tell you. On this second trip, Joe Bomb drove in with his own car from West Germany, a Pontiac."

"Are you sure about all this?" said the lieutenant. "Did you confirm that the girl has actually left Prague?"

"That wasn't necessary, comrade," said the sergeant, and then, still stinging from the recent unprecedented reprimand, added quickly, "Comrade lieutenant, Comrade Novotny was asked to keep track of what went on at the

Blazeks. And Comrade Novotny died at the hand of a murderer. A murderer who knew karate."

"He obviously tried to restrain Bomb," Malek piped up timidly, "and paid the consequences. We'll call Interior in on this, won't we? I mean, it goes beyond our mandate now."

"Wait a minute!" the lieutenant intervened, standing up. "Don't call anywhere."

"Why not?"

"This does not go beyond our mandate," declared the lieutenant in a mournful voice. "Bomb is a . . . a murderer," he said wearily. "He killed Novotny. And that's our job— to catch murderers."

"But this is a clear case of air piracy!" objected the sergeant.

"That is the intent," said the lieutenant. "So far, though, only the crime of murder has actually been committed. And that falls within our mandate."

"I don't know, Josef," said Malek. "The comrades from Interior certainly wouldn't mind making the arrests for us. Even though it's debatable who should do what."

"Of course they wouldn't mind," said the lieutenant. "But we're bound by oath. It's our *responsibility* to do everything in our power to arrest *anyone* who commits murder." Out of the corner of his eye, he saw the sergeant's face, which showed signs of an inner struggle. He resorted to a dishonorable ruse: "And then, comrades," he said, in a voice that sounded unnatural to his own ears, though they may have been oversensitive, "haven't you got just a little ambition? Aren't you even slightly proud to belong to a unit that is about to capture a criminal who not only murdered a comrade, but is getting ready to kidnap a *Czech* child and spirit her away to the West?"

"I think the main issue here is cooperation between the different branches," Malek objected feebly. The lieutenant, however, experienced a sensation of fleeting triumph, for the sergeant went for the bait.

"That's a fact, all right," Pudil declared. "We might even look at it as a kind of socialist competition. The murderer is ours, the air pirates belong to the comrades from Interior, as long as no weapons are used. But that's their problem, isn't it? If they're not vigilant and alert enough to come to the correct conclusions by themselves, why should we pass the ball to them when we can score the goal ourselves and at the same time stop those birds from flying the coop?"

"Let's go then," said Lieutenant Boruvka.

And they went.

THEY WENT. THE lieutenant didn't even have time to say goodbye to Zuzana and his wife. He merely called to tell them he wouldn't be home that night, which was nothing unusual in the old detective's family.

And then they went. Down a long highway undulating across hilltops beneath the stars, winding among silvery-green meadows that sparkled with diamond dew. A large moon hung over the countryside, as round as the lieutenant's face and, that night, just as pale. As pale as a white skull. Not the one from Edgar Allan Poe's fantasy, but one from the lieutenant's own experience. They drove past wheatfields golden in the daytime, the color of gold now, at night, waving in the night breeze beneath the cherry trees that lined the road. They drove through woods where the black shadows of magnificent owls flitted among the trees. A moth landed on the lieutenant's nose, then flew away; the sergeant, hunched over the wheel of the Volga, pushed the motor to the limit and the lieutenant's loaded pistol dug into his hip. The countryside sped by the open windows, redolent of barns and manure piles, villages submerged in darkness and silence, a landscape of clover and alfalfa, the lieu-

tenant's landscape, with ponds reflecting a twisted
moon, like the crumpled collages of one of those artists
from the Dubcek era who later committed suicide—an
ordinary suicide from an era of normalization. A landscape of fireflies and old, ancient history, a countryside
where criminals were drawn and quartered at a time
when the city of Memphis no longer existed and did
not yet exist. A large vampire bat dipped across the
stars. They stopped for a piss, as the sergeant put it.
They urinated into a ditch at the side of the road where
purple thistles grew; a large family of hedgehogs filed
across the road, the lieutenant said his farewells, and
they got back into the car.

Again they drove, rising and descending, along the
narrow highway, along the umbilical cord of life, soon to
be severed. The landscape smelled of darkness, of stars, of
spruce trees, of ponds, of old-fashioned train stations, of
the moon—and they were silent, the landscape possessed

by darkness. Some lines of poetry surfaced in the lieutenant's aching mind and they had a meaning, though he
did not know what; he only sensed it was bad. Memories
tempting him back into the saddle, that procession from
his past, the girls with the bloody breasts who, it was
decided in higher places, had been murdered by an
unknown assailant, the dancer with the sad slippers with a
hopeless four-leaf clover clinging to them who, it was
decided in higher places, had died of accidental asphyxia-
tion by natural gas. And what, then, do those higher
places leave in hands other than their own? Nothing? We
needn't be here at all, then. The foolish, wizened little
informer killed by a karate blow to the neck, humiliated
people who trustingly accept an offer of new pride, the
receding landscape, trees pregnant with fruit swaying above
the lurching Volga. . . . The lieutenant caught his head in
his hands and said to Malek, "Pavel, you don't happen to
have an aspirin with you, by any chance?"

AT FOUR IN the morning they drove into Resetice. The lieutenant phoned Mydloves from the police station. The local cop, who hadn't slept all night, confirmed that Bomb had arrived at the Cermaks' before midnight and carried the sleeping girl out of his car. The old detective issued the appropriate orders, then they left the Volga in Resetice and set off on foot down an overgrown track through the fields for the Mydloves airfield, about four kilometers away. It was getting light. A pale sliver on the eastern horizon slowly flared, expanded, and golden rays of light from the still-hidden sun shot through the pink clouds. At 5:30 they reached the airfield. It was a flat, uplands meadow, the grass cut short, with a narrow strip of concrete, an air sock, and, at the end of the runway, a wooden hangar. They knocked. The sleepy cop from Mydloves greeted them in the doorway.

"Nothing so far," he whispered. "They haven't shown

up yet." The lieutenant went inside and peered through a small window. Beyond the airfield the land fell away towards the village, beige and white in the early morning light. Above the village stood the white tower of a little church, topped with a red onion dome. A flock of quail flew out of the field, a swallow dipped and swirled over the meadow flushed pink with clover blossoms. A rooster crowed in the village, driving off death. Cows mooed. They heard an urban droning sound.

"Careful," whispered Pudil, standing behind the lieutenant. There was a faint click as he disengaged the safety catch on his weapon. The local copy looked nervously at him and then squinted at the lieutenant.

"Are we going to use guns?"

"Not you, under any circumstances," said the lieutenant. "This is our business."

The sound grew louder and a car appeared on the narrow track through the field. It was a big, beige, two-tone American Pontiac, with a coffee-colored roof, lurching along the path like a drunken ship. It stopped at the edge of the narrow concrete runway. An enormous man in a wide-brimmed hat stepped out and looked at his watch. He was tall, like the hero in a cowboy movie. The sun, just edging over the horizon, shone on his head. The man looked around and the lieutenant saw a bronzed, creased face that reminded him of illustrations in the old novels by Cooper he'd read as a child.

"Bomb!" whispered the sergeant.

The lieutenant merely nodded.

The man glanced at his watch again, then leaned over to say something to someone in the car. In the window of the Pontiac was the silhouette of a woman in a babushka. The man stepped away from the car, positioned himself at the end of the concrete runway, and stood with his legs apart.

The sun came up, the pink clouds faded to white, the fields on the opposite hillside sparkled gold. It was silent except for the chirping of awakening crickets and the chatter of birds. The swallow was performing low-level acrobatics again over the runway.

Then they heard another faint droning sound. The enormous man tipped his hat farther down his forehead to shade his eyes from the rising sun. The droning increased; a dot appeared in the blue sky and grew until it was recognizable as a small, blue airplane. The man raised both hands. The plane banked, then leveled and began its approach, pointing its nose straight at the end of the runway. It descended, flared, its wheels touched the concrete. The man remained with his arms outstretched while the plane taxied up to him. Then he ran to the car. The aircraft came to a halt, someone inside threw back the bubble canopy, and the head of a young man in a flying helmet appeared. The lieutenant recognized him.

But still he remained silent.

"Comrade lieutenant! Let's nail 'em," whispered Sergeant Pudil nervously.

The old detective gave out a sound like a groan, but Sergeant Pudil interpreted it in his own way. Briskly he threw open the hangar door and, with his pistol drawn, ran out onto the airfield. The man in the wide-brimmed hat, with the little girl in his arms, was just turning around. He saw the sergeant and started running towards the plane in long, loping strides.

"Halt!" roared the sergeant. The plane began turning around. "You too!" The sergeant pointed to the pilot with his left hand. "One move and I'll shoot you all! Comrade lieutenant!"

Malek ran out of the hangar and slowly, almost embarrassedly, pulled out his pistol. He looked around at the lieutenant.

"You take care of the pilot," the sergeant shrieked at

Malek, "and you, put that kid down!"

The man in the wide-brimmed hat stopped, hesitated.

"Make it snappy or I'll shoot! Comrade lieutenant, where are you?"

In the hangar, Lieutenant Boruvka came to his senses. He looked around and saw the village cop standing there awkwardly. Several buttons on his shirt were undone. The lieutenant drew his pistol and pointed it at him.

"Give me your pistol," he commanded. "Come on! That's an order!"

The policeman fumbled with his holster and uncertainly handed the lieutenant his gun.

The old detective walked out of the hangar. The sergeant looked round at him and said, less loudly now, "Good! You cover him while I search him for weapons, comrade lieutenant." He stuck his own pistol into his holster and walked up to the man in the wide-brimmed hat.

"Stay where you are," said the lieutenant. His voice was scarcely audible. Sergeant Pudil stopped abruptly, then looked around in alarm, as though he'd been caught off guard by someone else entering the game.

"Yes, you," said the lieutenant, aiming the pistol in his right hand at the sergeant's chest. "And you, Pavel, throw down your gun," he told Malek, aiming the second pistol at him.

"Josef, come on," said Malek uncertainly.

The sergeant stared from one to the other in astonishment. Then he shouted at Malek, "Shoot! This is sabotage!"

"Come on, Josef, don't be crazy," said Malek nervously.

"I'm not crazy, Pavel. I'm deadly serious. Throw down your gun."

The man in the wide-brimmed hat watched everything with dangerously calm eyes.

"Get serious, Josef, You can't . . ."

"I will if . . . if I have to, Pavel. Please don't make me. . . ."

Slowly, Lieutenant Malek let his arm fall and dropped the pistol into the grass. The old detective knew—and it warmed his heart for an instant—that Malek hadn't done it because he feared for his life. The enormous man's eyes flashed. He bent down quickly, grabbed the child, who had begun to cry, and was at the plane in several long strides. The young man in the flying helmet leaned out of the cockpit and lifted the child inside.

"Quick!" the man called to the lieutenant. "Come on! It's a two-seater. There's room for two *and* the kid."

The lieutenant shook his head. "You get in!"

"No, you go. Give me the guns. I can look after myself!"

Once more the lieutenant shook his head. "No you can't. Get in! There's not much time!"

"You're risking your neck, man!"

"So are you," said the lieutenant. "And my family still lives here."

The man in the wide-brimmed hat hesitated a moment longer. His bronzed face, creased with the marks of a different, more violent experience than the lieutenant's, was lit by the morning sun.

"Get a move on!" said the old detective.

For another brief moment the man looked at the Pontiac where the country woman with the kerchief on her head sat shyly, then back at the lieutenant. "Okay," he said. "Good luck, pardner."

He swung himself up into the cockpit. The plexiglass canopy snapped shut, the engine roared as the plane swung round and accelerated along the concrete runway. It lurched heavily into the air and rose slowly over the field of clover towards the west. They could see it a while longer, then it dipped over the woods and was gone.

The sergeant let his hands fall. "I can't believe this. . . ."

"Keep your hands up," said the lieutenant. "We have to wait at least a half an hour. It's thirty kilometers to the border. I hope they fly low enough to avoid the radar." Then he grinned. It was a sad grin, without a trace of irony. "Just like those Zionists. Remember, Pudil!"

THE YOUNG—OR rather, not so young, but still attractive—blonde woman in bell-bottomed trousers and a honey-colored sweater stood respectfully in front of an overweight man who slouched in a chair behind his desk, picking at his teeth with a toothpick.

"No, we're not related," she was saying, "but we were friends for many years. That counts for something, doesn't it?"

"Only immediate family have the right to a visit. Wives, children . . ."

"His wife died when—when it happened. She had a stroke."

"Does that surprise you, comrade?" said the man, examining a piece of meat he had pried out of his teeth.

"No, it doesn't. But the fact is, she died and we . . . we were planning to get married."

The man looked at her derisively. "That's not something I'd go around advertising. She died after they arrested him."

"What I mean to say is," said the blonde woman, "that I'd like to marry him. If that's possible."

"It's not," said the man, "and it won't be for another fifteen years. And anyway, who knows," he went on, looking her up and down, "if you'll still want to marry him then. He'll be sixty-seven when he gets out."

The blonde pouted contemptuously.

"Unless he keeps his nose clean," said the man, "and there's a political amnesty. But don't hold your breath. It's going to take us some time to clean up the moral havoc wreaked by people like him."

"He didn't wreak any moral havoc."

"He aided and abetted an act of air piracy," said the man. "And he was lucky he did it before the National Assembly brought back the rope. Otherwise—" he grinned insolently "—you wouldn't be able to marry him, not even when you turn," and again he ran his eyes over the woman's trim figure, "fifty or whatever."

"A hundred and fifty," said the blonde, returning his insolent sneer. "So you won't let me see him?"

"Out of the question," said the man. "Who do you think you are? The law applies to everyone. You're wasting my time."

He looked directly into her eyes. She stared back at him defiantly.

"Unless," said the man, and he looked around, took his phone off the hook, and lowered his voice, "unless some exceptional reasons were offered. Do you know what I mean?" He ran his eyes over her again, from the bell-bottomed trousers, up her slender thighs and her shapely breasts, to her large mouth and gray eyes.

The blonde woman looked at him disdainfully. "In that case, I'd just as soon forget about it, even though it tears my heart out. If you know what a heart is."

The man lowered his voice even more. "Come on, lady! Surely its worth two grand, isn't it? Or are you going to stand there and tell me you'll wait fifteen years? You're no spring chicken yourself."

THE WOMAN WAS uncertain whether it had really been worth the two grand, which took a hefty slice out of her modest savings. The lieutenant—of course he was a lieutenant no longer—was brought into the large, gray unpleasant visiting room. They sat him down opposite her, with a thick wire mesh between them. The old detective was wearing clothes made of the kind of cloth they make cheap rugs from. She had feared the encounter, but was encouraged when she saw that the lieutenant's round face had not aged. On the contrary, it almost seemed to her that it had grown younger. In any case, it was calm. The blue eyes looked at her through the wire mesh, and a deep, tender friendship radiated from them.

Like everyone else in this situation, they didn't know what to talk about, so they merely chatted. The lieutenant told her how much he regretted the fact that Malek had been demoted to constable for not using his weapon, though they hadn't discharged him because he had claimed that he simply couldn't believe his eyes, and they had treated that as an extenuating circumstance. The sergeant was promoted to first lieutenant. The Blazeks, out of consideration for their advanced age, were sentenced to three years each, and Mrs. Cermak and her husband got five. Joe Bomb was given the noose in absentia and the state prosecutor requested his extradition from the United States. The request was turned down. So they confiscated the Pontiac. In the glove compartment they found an American Express card, and this led Pudil off on a long wild-goose chase through the archives of the Ministry of the Interior, but he never did manage to find even a trace of Zionism clinging to the name Bambasek.

Then the singer spoke. She had managed to make a kind of comeback. A certain Kopanec, a writer who, though blacklisted, still had influential contacts, had written a television program about her under the pseudonym of a trusted Party member. The program had gone down well, and now she was touring with Vaclav Hybs's group, mainly to Bulgaria, the Soviet Union, and occasionally Cuba. Perhaps one day they'd go to Chile too. She saw that the lieutenant was pleased by the news, but then he grew sad. Cuba, he said. That was almost in America. "And they've definitely turned down Zuzana's application to leave," he said. "But you know how it is, Eve. Her husband's in the States. In Memphis, Tennessee. That's what makes me feel worst of all. You know how it is. She's my daughter."

"POOR DAD," SAID Zuzana. They were sitting by an open window; it was the month when cats make love and the velvet cavaliers, suspecting nothing about the world and its changeable laws, sang their unchanging song across the tile rooftops. "I can tell you now, Eve. I know you and Father were having an affair, but it doesn't bother me. Perhaps there's some kind of cosmic justice in it."

"I'm ashamed," said the blonde. "But you know yourself how helpless you can feel in a situation like that."

"I do," said Zuzana. "Did you know he's not my real father?"

The blond woman was astonished. "You're kidding!"

"See my eyes?" said Zuzana, opening her very pretty green eyes for the singer to see.

"Yes?"

"And have you noticed what color father's eyes are?"

"Of course," said the blonde. "Forget-me-not blue."

"And mother's were gray."

"And?"

"So practically speaking, it's impossible," said Zuzana. "A blue-eyed man and a gray-eyed woman, if they stood on their heads, could never give birth to a creature like me."

Both women were silent. On the rooftops, the eternal tomcats sang their song.

"But he's my father all the same," said Zuzana. "I couldn't have had a better one. Even though in the end he . . . no, he didn't screw up. Father didn't screw anything up. It was the others who did that—the bastards!"

THEY LAY IN each other's arms, the blond woman and the girl with green eyes, and they wept until the moon came out and the tomcats fell silent.

"Can I stay the night?" asked the blonde woman.

"Sure. We'll sleep here in my parents' bed."

Lying beside each other and staring into the darkness, the blonde said, "He told me—when we were saying goodbye—something very strange. I don't understand what he meant."

"What was it?"

"He said that no matter how it was and no matter whether he did a good thing or not, he said, at least some fish or other died. From the Paraná River. Do you know what he was talking about?"

"No, I don't," said Zuzana. "He never told me anything like that."

They stared into the darkness for a long time. Then they fell asleep. On the other side of the city, the former lieutenant slept on a wooden cot, sleeping the deep, dreamless sleep of people who, though they may be misguided, are kind and honorable.

Janet Malcolm

A NIGHT IN PRAGUE

PRAGUE IS A small town, easy to find one's way around in. On learning that it was also entirely safe, I had been enjoying solitary walks at night through cobbled streets so empty and silent that one could hear one's foot-steps. Tonight, before turning off the Smetana embank-ment and heading toward my hotel, near Wenceslas

---

Journalist Janet Malcolm is perhaps best known for her feud with Freud scholar Jeffrey Masson. Despite the latter's allegations of unsubstantiated reporting, Malcolm is widely respected and known for her in-depth mag-azine essays. This excerpt is from a 1990 New Yorker portrait of modern Prague.

Square, I crossed the street and gazed up at Hradčany, the Prague Castle, rising from the far bank of the river like a mystical vision. The castle is actually a collection of medieval and Renaissance structures—palaces, residences, churches, chapels—dominated by St. Vitus' Cathedral, one of the great Gothic cathedrals of Europe, which was now bathed in a delicate blue-green light. The surrounding buildings, which included the Presidential palace, were illuminated by a golden light. Willows and fruit trees about to flower grew on the riverbank, forming the foreground of this ravishing night picture. I stood leaning against the balustrade of the embankment promenade, utterly alone, and feeling the special joy that adventitious aesthetic experience brings. Then my eye fell on a disagreeable sight on the riverbank below me. Glaring whitely out of the darkness was a disorderly pile of papers that someone had left strewn about on the grass. The sight of litter, unpleasing anywhere, is positively arresting in clean, orderly Prague. There is no refuse in Prague's streets, no windblown newspapers, no bottles, no dirty rags, no candy wrappers, no half-eaten pieces of pizza. During my previous visit, hundreds of thousands of people gathered in Wenceslas Square on New Year's Eve to celebrate the beginning of the post-Communist era, and thousands of bottles of champagne were drunk and then either smashed or left standing on the street in merry circles around the trees lining the square and in rows along the edges of the sidewalk. (Wenceslas Square is actually a long, wide boulevard of hotels, shops, cafés, and restaurants, with a statue of the Saint on horseback at its uphill end.) On New Year's Day, between eight in the morning and noon, volunteer bands of citizens gathered in the square with twig brooms, swept up the broken glass, and helped load it and the thousands of bottles into city garbage trucks, so that by noon the square was completely restored to order and no trace remained of the revelry of the night before.

As I stared with displeasure at the papers strewn on the riverbank, they underwent a transformation before my eyes and turned into the white feathers of a swan sitting on a nest she had unaccountably chosen to build on the grass just below the promenade. She gleamed out of the darkness, curving her neck and pecking at herself with affected unconcern, aware of me but sitting tight. When I looked up, the cathedral was gone. The blue-green light had been extinguished, and now only the buildings in the foreground were visible; one could make out, if one knew where to look, the faintest trace of the cathedral spires. Then the golden light went out, too, and the whole vision disappeared. I moved on.

A little street off the embankment turned out to lead to the Theatre on the Balustrade, where a performance of Havel's "Largo Desolato" was just letting out. Havel wrote this play—about a dissident leader who is having a nervous breakdown—in 1984, a year and a half after his release from a three-and-a-half year prison term. It had been circulated in samizdat, and had been produced in Germany and America but never in Czechoslovakia. Havel came to work at the Theatre on the Balustrade as a stage-hand in 1960, and soon became one of the shaping forces of its mordant, ironic spirit. It was here that he found his voice as a playwright; while associated with the theatre, he wrote "The Garden Party," "The Memorandum," and "The Increased Difficulty of Concentration," the absurdist plays on which his international reputation was based. The theatre's great period—during which Jarry's "Ubu Roi," Beckett's "Waiting for Godot," Ionesco's one-act plays, and Havel's plays were produced, among others—coincided with the period of liberalization in Czechoslovakia that abruptly ended in August, 1968, with the arrival of Russian tanks. (Havel left the theatre shortly after the Russian invasion—for nonpolitical reasons, he has reported, though obviously, he further notes, he couldn't have lasted under the new dispensation, given "my various extra-theatrical activities.") In the autobiographical "Disturbing the Peace," a book of essayistic responses to questions sent him in 1985 by Karel Hvížďala, a Czech journalist then living in exile in West Germany, Havel traces the history of the Theatre on the Balustrade and that of other small, avant-garde Prague theatres of the sixties. "Life in Prague was different then," he observes. "Prague had not yet been buried under a landslide of general apathy and turned stiff and corpse-like under its weight. In other words—paradoxically—it made sense to deal with the absurdity of being, because things still mattered." After 1968, the Theatre on the Balustrade, though retaining high standards of production and performance, lost its radical edge, as did every other cultural institution tolerated by the regime.

On the afternoon of December 31, 1989, I had been at a party held in the anteroom of the Theatre on the

Balustrade, at which many of the leading writers, artists, academics, and theatre people of Prague were present, including Havel himself. He is a man of chunky build who looks younger than in his pictures and has a most winningly natural manner. He came to the party dressed in dark-gray denim jeans and a dark-blue sweater over a white shirt. He spoke softly, sincerely, easily to the people who approached him, drinking a beer, chain-smoking, gesturing a lot, often breaking into a wonderful smile. In his autobiographical writings (and, indirectly, in his plays) Havel has shown doubt-filled, anguished, neurotic sides of himself, but his public persona is that of a man who is remarkably comfortable with himself and knows how to be simple and direct without ever being glib. "Fortunately, my nature is such that I get on well with everyone," he wrote to his wife, Olga, while he was in detention in a crowded cell in the Prague Ruzyně jail, adding significantly, "And I'm able to suppress my various emotions." In the crowded cell of public life that Havel now inhabits, his gifts of self-control must serve him as well as they served him when he was incarcerated among murderers and thieves.

That New Year's Eve, I got another glimpse of Havel at a glittering party given by the Civic Forum, to which the whole Prague opposition movement and its members in exile had been invited. The atmosphere was something like that of an art opening in SoHo combined with a wedding in Astoria. People sat at long tables in an enormous hall drinking champagne and happily listening to a terrible rock band. Just before midnight, Havel, wearing a suit, appeared on a stage, received an ecstatic ovation, and, in reply to a request for a speech, said good-humoredly, "I must remind you that what we are starting here is a democracy, not a monarchy." At midnight, the national anthem was played, and everyone stood up to sing and to cry. So much communal good feeling is rarely encountered, and on my second visit to Prague I was not encountering it. The city was sinking into what the critic Tzvetan Todorov has called "post-totalitarian depression"—a condition whose pathos was somehow only deepened by the hordes of tourists pouring into it.

I CONTINUED MY night walk through small, empty, winding streets and then along Národní Třída, a wide thoroughfare, where I was joined by a few other strollers. I passed the place where on November 17, 1989, the police had savagely beaten peacefully demonstrating students with truncheons—the so-called massacre that roused the traditionally supine Czechs to action. Where Národní Třída approaches Wenceslas Square stands a handsome white six-story Art Nouveau building, which became the headquarters of the Civic Forum soon after its elegant rout of the Communists. (The Civic Forum's original headquarters had been the subterranean Magic Lantern Theatre.) Street musicians had begun to perform in the open plaza in front of the building—under the Communists, street music was forbidden, as was another recently introduced Prague entertainment: *striptýz*—and when I arrived at the plaza an unusually large crowd was gathered around a pair of folk-rock singers, a young man and a young woman singing to the accompaniment of the young man's guitar. However, what had attracted the crowd was not the singing and playing, which were unremarkable, but an oddity: a very old woman, resembling one of the poor deranged creatures one sees wandering about the Upper West Side, had attached herself to the singers and was hopping about after them in a bizarre parody of rock dancing. The crowd laughed in a careless, good-natured way. The cruelty of the spectacle was blunted by the geniality of the performers; the pretty, rose-cheeked girl smiled encouragingly at the old woman and treated her more as a co-performer than as a freakish interloper. Earlier in the day, I had seen a crowd in Wenceslas

Square gathered around another curiosity, this one a small demonstration that called itself a Protestní Žranice. ("Pig-Out Protest" is the best I can do.) The protest took the form of a free distribution of food and drink to passersby: anyone who would accept them was handed a huge pallid hunk of boiled chicken wrapped in foil, a piece of bread, a slab of salami, and a beer. What was being protested, I learned from a man biting into his chicken, was the Communist Party's retention of money and property. The protestor-distributors were some sort of ad-hoc group, which wasn't running candidates in the coming election but—as my informant described it—"just does things for fun." The Protestní Žranice was evidently a takeoff on the Protestní Hladovka—hunger strike.

Back at the hotel, I turned on the television to one of the two Czech channels, which was showing a film about Robert Schumann and Clara Wieck. (Clara: "Did you write that?" Robert: "Unfortunately no. Heine.") I investigated the other channel, which was broadcasting an interview with a young athlete who had won a prize in Athens ("How did you like Athens, Jiří?" "Very dirty. It's better in pictures"); switched back to Schumann (Mendelssohn: "Have more faith, Schumann"), back to the athlete ("What are your plans for the future, Jiří?" "To go on as before"); and finally alighted on a hazy but riveting "Swan Lake" from the Bolshoi on the Russian channel.

Jaroslav Hasek

THE GOOD SOLDIER SCHWEIK

THERE WERE THREE passengers in a second-class compartment of the Prague-Budejovice express. Lieutenant Lukash, opposite whom an elderly and entirely bald gentleman was sitting, and Schweik, who was standing modestly in the corridor and was just preparing to listen to a fresh storm of abuse from Lieutenant Lukash who, regardless of

---

*Jaroslav Hasek's participation in World War I convinced him of the utter stupidity of war. As a result, he began what was to be his lifelong work: a ruthless satire, an incredibly popular yet unfinished novel—*The Good Soldier Schweik *(1930).*

the presence of the bald-headed civilian, kept yelling at Schweik throughout the journey, that he was a God-forsaken idiot and similar things.

The cause of the trouble was a trifling matter, a slight discrepancy in the number of pieces of luggage that Schweik was looking after.

"One of our trunks has been stolen, you say," snarled the lieutenant at Schweik. "That's a fine thing to tell anyone, you jackass. What was in that trunk?"

"Nothing at all, sir," replied Schweik, with his eyes glued to the bald head of the civilian, who was sitting opposite to the lieutenant, and who appeared to be taking no interest whatever in the matter, but was reading the *Neue Freie Presse.* "All that was in that trunk was a looking-glass from the bedroom and an iron clothes hanger from the passage, so that we didn't really lose anything, because the looking-glass and the hanger belonged to the landlord."

"Shut up, Schweik," the lieutenant shouted. "I'll deal

with you when we get to Budejovice. Do you know I'm going to have you locked up?"

"Beg to report, sir, I don't," said Schweik blandly. "You never mentioned anything to me about it before, sir."

The lieutenant gritted his teeth, sighed, took a copy of the *Bohemia* from his pocket and began to read news about great victories, and the exploits of the German submarine "E" in the Mediterranean. Just when he had come to a report about a new German invention for blowing cities up by means of special triple detonating bombs dropped from aeroplanes, he was interrupted by the voice of Schweik, who was addressing the bald-headed gentleman:

"Excuse me, guv'nor, but ain't you Mr. Purkrábek, agent of the Slavia Bank?"

When the bald-headed gentleman made no reply, Schweik said to the lieutenant:

"Beg to report, sir, I once read in the paper that the

average man has 60,000 to 70,000 hairs on his head and that many examples show black hair is thinner as a rule."

And he continued remorselessly:

"Then there was a doctor who said that loss of hair was due to mental disturbance during confinements."

But now a dreadful thing happened. The bald-headed gentleman jumped towards Schweik and shouted: "Get out of here, you dirty swine," and having hustled him into the corridor, returned to the carriage, where he gave the lieutenant a little surprise by introducing himself.

Evidently there had been a mistake. The bald-headed man was not Mr. Purkrábek, agent of the Slavia Bank, but merely Major-General von Schwarzburg. The major-general was just proceeding in mufti on a series of garrison inspections and was now about to pay a surprise visit to Budejovice.

He was the most fearsome major-general who had ever walked the earth, and if he found anything amiss, the following dialogue would ensue between him and the garrison commandant:

"Have you got a revolver?"

"Yes, sir."

"All right, then. If I were in your place, I'd know what to do with it. This isn't a garrison, it's a pigsty."

And, as a matter of fact, there were always a certain number who shot themselves after one of his inspections, whereupon Major-General von Schwarzburg would always observe with satisfaction:

"That's the style! That's what I call a soldier."

He now said to Lieutenant Lukash:

"Where did you attend the cadet school?"

"At Prague."

"So you attended a cadet school and are not aware that an officer is responsible for his subordinate? That's a nice state of affairs. And then you carry on a conversation with your orderly as if he were a close friend of yours.

You allow him to talk without being asked. That's an even nicer state of affairs. In the third place, you allow him to insult your superior officers. And that caps all. What is your name?

"Lukash."

"And what regiment are you in?"

"I was—"

"I'm not asking where you were but where you are."

"In the 91st regiment, sir. They transferred me—"

"Oh, they transferred you, did they? Quite right, too. It won't do you any harm to get to the front as soon as possible with the 91st regiment."

"That's already settled, sir."

The major-general now held a lecture about how, of recent years, he had observed that officers talk to their subordinates in a familiar manner, and this he held to be a dangerous tendency, inasmuch as it promoted the spread of democratic principles. The private soldier must keep himself to himself, he must tremble before his superior officer, he must fear him. Officers must keep the rank-and-file at a distance of ten paces from them and not allow them to think independently or, indeed, to think at all. There was a time when officers put the fear of God into the rank-and-file, but nowadays—

The major-general made a hopeless gesture with his hand.

"Nowadays the majority of officers absolutely coddle the rank-and-file. That's all I wanted to say."

The major-general picked up his newspaper again and engrossed himself in it. Lieutenant Lukash, as white as a sheet, went out into the corridor to settle accounts with Schweik.

He found him by the window, looking as blissful and contented as a baby a month old who has drunk its fill and is now dropping off to sleep.

The lieutenant stopped, beckoned to Schweik and

pointed to an empty compartment. He entered at Schweik's heels and closed the door.

"Schweik," he said solemnly, "the time has now come for you to get the biggest hiding on record. What on earth did you interfere with that bald-headed gentleman for? Do you know that he's Major-General von Schwarzburg?"

"Beg to report, sir," announced Schweik, with the air of a martyr, "never in my life have I had the least intention of insulting anyone and it's news to me about him being a major-general. As true as I stand here, he's the living image of Mr. Purkrábek, agent of the Slavia Bank. He used to come to our pub and once, when he fell asleep at a table, some joker wrote on his bald head with a copying ink pencil: 'Please note our scheme for safeguarding your children's future as per schedule IIIc enclosed.' "

After a short pause, Schweik continued:

"There was no need for that gentleman to get into such a wax over a little mistake like that. It's an absolute fact he's supposed to have 60,000 to 70,000 hairs, like the average man has, just as the article said. It never struck me there was such a thing as a bald-headed major-general. Well, that's what they call a tragic mistake, the same as anybody might make when he passes a remark and somebody else takes it in a wrong way without giving him a chance to explain. I used to know a tailor who—"

Lieutenant Lukash gave one more look at Schweik and then left the compartment. He returned to his former seat, and after a few minutes Schweik's guileless countenance appeared in the doorway:

"Beg to report, sir, we'll be at Tábor in five minutes. The train stops there for five minutes. Wouldn't you care to order a little snack or something? Years and years ago they used to have very good—"

The lieutenant jumped up furiously and in the corridor he said to Schweik:

"Let me tell you once more that the less I see of you, the better I shall like it. If I had my way I'd never set eyes on you again, and you can take it from me that I won't if I can damn well help it. Don't let me see anything of you. Keep out of my sight, you blithering jackass, you."

"Very good, sir."

Schweik saluted, turned smartly to the right-about, in the military manner, and then went to the end of the corridor, where he sat down in a corner on the guard's seat and entered into a conversation with a railwayman.

"There's a question I'd like to ask you, boss."

The railwayman, who evidently was in no mood for conversation, nodded listlessly.

"I used to know a chap named Hofmann," began Schweik, "and he always made out that these alarm signals never act, what I mean to say, that nothing would happen if you pulled this handle. To tell you the honest truth, I never gave the matter another thought, but as soon as I spotted this alarm outfit here, I thought I'd like to know what's what, in case I should ever need it."

Schweik stood up and accompanied the railwayman to the alarm brake marked: "In case of danger."

The railwayman considered it his duty to explain to Schweik exactly what the alarm mechanism consisted of.

"He was right when he said you've got to pull this here handle, but he was kidding you when he made out it don't act. The train always stops, because this is connected with all the carriages and the engine. The alarm brake is bound to act."

While he was saying this, they both had their hands on the handle of the lever and then—how it happened must remain a mystery—they pulled it and the train stopped.

They were quite unable to agree as to who had actually done it and made the alarm signal work.

Schweik declared that he couldn't have done it.

"It's a fair marvel to me," he said good-humoredly to

the guard, "why the train stopped so sudden. It was going, then all at once it stopped. I'm more upset about it than what you are."

A solemn gentleman took the guard's part and said he'd heard the soldier start a conversation about alarm signals.

On the other hand, Schweik kept harping upon his good name and insisted that it was no advantage to him for the train to be late, because he was on his way to the front.

"The station master'll tell you all about it," declared the guard. "This'll cost you twenty crowns."

Meanwhile the passengers could be seen climbing down from the carriages, the head guard blew a whistle, and a lady in a panic started running with a portmanteau across the railway track into the fields. "It's well worth twenty crowns, that it is," said Schweik stolidly, maintaining complete composure. "It's cheap at the price."

Just then the head guard joined the audience.

"Well, it's about time we made a move," said Schweik. "It's a nuisance when a train's late. If it was in peace time it wouldn't matter so much, but now that there's a war on, all the trains are carrying troops, major-generals, lieutenants, orderlies. It's a risky business being late like that. Napoleon was five minutes late at Waterloo and, emperor or no emperor, he got himself into a mess just the same."

At this moment Lieutenant Lukash pushed his way through the group. He was ghastly pale and all he could utter was the word "Schweik!"

Schweik saluted and explained: "Beg to report, sir, they're making out I stopped the train. The railway company have got very funny plugs on their emergency brakes. It's better to keep away from them or else something'll go wrong and they'll ask you to fork out twenty crowns, the same as they're asking me."

The head guard had already blown his whistle and the train was starting again. The passengers returned to their seats, and Lieutenant Lukash, without another word, also went back to his compartment.

The guard now called upon Schweik to pay a fine of twenty crowns, as otherwise he would have to take him before the station master at Tábor.

"That's all right," said Schweik. "I like talking to educated people. It'll be a fair treat for me to see that station master at Tábor."

When the train arrived at Tábor, Schweik with all due ceremony went to Lieutenant Lukash and said:

"Beg to report, sir, I'm being taken before the station master."

Lieutenant Lukash did not reply. He had become completely indifferent to everything. It struck him that the best thing he could do was not to care a rap about anybody, whether it was Schweik or the bald-headed major-general, and to sit quietly where he was, to leave the train at Budejovice, to report himself at the barracks and to proceed to the front with a draft. At the front, if the worst came to the worst, he would be killed and thus get away from this appalling world in which such monstrosities as Schweik were knocking about.

When the train started again, Lieutenant Lukash looked out of the window and saw Schweik standing on the platform and engrossed in a solemn colloquy with the station master. Schweik was surrounded by a crowd of people in which several railway uniforms were visible.

Lieutenant Lukash heaved a sigh. It was not a sigh of pity. His heart felt lighter at the thought that Schweik had been left behind on the platform. Even the bald-headed major-general did not seem to be quite such a horrid bugbear.

The train had long since puffed its way into Budejovice, but there was no diminution in the crowd round Schweik.

Schweik was asserting his innocence, and had so convinced the assembly that one lady remarked:

"They're bullying another soldier again."

The assembly accepted this view, and a gentleman announced to the station master that he was prepared to pay Schweik's fine for him. He was convinced that the soldier had not done what he was accused of.

Then a police sergeant made his appearance and, having grabbed hold of a man in the crowd, led him away, saying:

"What d'you mean by causing all this disturbance? If that's the way you want soldiers treated, how d'you expect Austria to win the war?"

Meanwhile, the worthy person who believed in Schweik's innocence had paid the fine for him and had taken Schweik into the third-class refreshment room, where he had treated him to a beer. And having ascertained that all his papers, including his railway warrant, were in the possession of Lieutenant Lukash, he generously presented him with the sum of five crowns for a ticket and sundry expenses.

Schweik stayed where he was, and while he was quietly drinking his way through the five crowns, the people on the platform who had not witnessed Schweik's interview with the station master, and had only seen a crowd in the distance, were telling each other that a spy had been caught taking photographs of the railway station, but a lady contradicted this rumour by declaring that it wasn't a spy at all, but she had heard that a dragoon had struck an officer near the ladies' lavatory because the officer was following his (the dragoon's) sweetheart. These fantastic conjectures were brought to an end by the police, who cleared the platform. And Schweik went on quietly drinking; he wondered with a tender concern what Lieutenant Lukash had done when he reached Budejovice and found no signs of his orderly anywhere.

Before the departure of the slow train, the third-class

refreshment room became packed with travellers, consisting mostly of soldiers belonging to the most varied units and nationalities. The tide of war had swept them into hospital and now they were again leaving for the front to be wounded, mutilated and tortured once more, so as to qualify for a wooden cross on their graves.

"*Ihre Dokumente, vasi tokúment,*" a sergent-major of the military police now remarked to Schweik in German and broken Czech. He was accompanied by four soldiers with fixed bayonets. "You sit, *nicht fahren,* sit, drink, keep on drink," he continued in his elegant jargon.

"Haven't got none, *milacku,*"[1] replied Schweik. "Lieutenant Lukash of the 91st regiment took them with him and left me here in the station."

"*Was ist das Wort: milacek?*"[2] asked the sergeant-major, turning to one of his soldiers, an old defence corps man who replied:

---

[1] "Darling."
[2] "What does *milacek* mean?"

"Milacek, das ist wie: Herr Feldwebel."[1]

The sergeant-major continued his conversation with Schweik:

"Papers, every soldier, without papers, lock up."

They took Schweik accordingly to the military transport headquarters.

"It's no use, chum, you've got to get it over. So in you go," said the corporal to Schweik in a sympathetic tone.

And he led Schweik into an office where, behind a table littered with papers, sat a small lieutenant who looked exceedingly fierce. When he saw Schweik with the corporal, he remarked: "Aha!" in a significant manner. Whereupon the corporal explained:

"Beg to report, sir, this man was found in the station without any papers."

The lieutenant nodded as if to indicate that years and years ago he had guessed that precisely on that day and at

---

[1] *"Milacek,* that's the same as sergeant-major."

that hour Schweik would be found in the station without papers, for anyone looking at Schweik at that moment could not help feeling convinced that it was quite impossible for a man of such appearance and bearing to have any papers on him.

At last he asked:

"What were you doing in the station?"

"Beg to report, sir, I was waiting for the train to Budejovice, because I want to get to my regiment where I'm orderly to Lieutenant Lukash, but I got left behind on account of being taken to the station master to pay a fine through being suspected of stopping the express we were travelling in, by pulling the alarm signal."

"Here, I can't make head or tail of this," shouted the lieutenant. "Can't you say what you've got to say in a straightforward manner, without drivelling away like a lunatic?"

"Beg to report, sir, that from the first minute I sat

down with Lieutenant Lukash in that train that was to take us to our 91st imperial royal infantry regiment without any hanging about we had nothing but bad luck. First of all we lost a trunk, then by way of a change, there was a major-general, a bald-headed cove—"

"Oh, good Lord!" sighed the lieutenant.

And while the lieutenant fumed, Schweik continued:

"Well, somehow or other this bald-headed major-general got his knife into me at the very start, and Lieutenant Lukash, that's the officer I'm orderly to, he sent me out into the corridor. Then in the corridor I got accused of doing what I've told you. And while they were looking into it, I got left behind on the platform. The train was gone, the lieutenant with his trunks and his papers and with my papers was gone too, and there I was left in the lurch like an orphan, with no papers and no nothing."

Schweik gazed at the lieutenant with such a touching air of gentleness that the latter was quite convinced of the absolute truth of what he was hearing from the lips of this fellow who, to all appearances, was a congenital idiot. He now enumerated to Schweik all the trains which had left for Budejovice since the departure of the express, and he asked him why he had missed them as well.

"Beg to report, sir," replied Schweik, with a good-humoured smile, "that while I was waiting for the next train, I got into more trouble through having a few drinks."

"I've never seen such a fool," pondered the lieutenant. "He owns up to everything. I've had plenty of them here, and they all swear blind they've never done anything. But this chap comes up as cool as a cucumber and says: I lost all the trains through having a few drinks."

The lieutenant decided that the time had now come to settle the matter once and for all. He therefore said in emphatic tones:

"Now then, you blithering idiot, you fat-headed lout,

go to the booking-office, buy a ticket and clear off to Budejovice. If I see any more of you, I'll treat you as a deserter! Dismiss!

As Schweik did not move, but kept his hand at the salute at the peak of his cap, the lieutenant bellowed:

"Quick march outside, didn't you hear what I said? Corporal Palánek, take this drivelling idiot to the booking office and buy him a ticket to Budejovice."

After a short interval Corporal Palánek again appeared at the lieutenant's office. Behind Palánek, through the open door, peeped Schweik's good-humoured countenance.

"What is it now?"

"Beg to report sir," whispered Corporal Palánek mysteriously, "he's got no money for a ticket and I've got none, either. They won't let him ride free because he's got no papers to show he's going to the regiment."

The lieutenant promptly delivered a judgment of Solomon to settle the quandry.

"Then let him walk there," he decided, "and when he gets there they can shove him in the clink for being late. We can't be bothered with him here."

"It's no use, chum," said Corporal Palánek to Schweik when they were outside the office again, "you'll have to walk to Budejovice, old sport. We've got some bread rations in the guard room. I'll give you some to take with you."

And half an hour later, when they had treated Schweik to black coffee, and besides the bread rations had given him a packet of army tobacco to take with him to the regiment, he left Tábor at dead of night, singing an old army song. And heaven knows how it happened that the good soldier Schweik instead of turning southward towards Budejovice, went due west. He trudged through snow, wrapped up in his army greatcoat, like the last of Napoleon's guards returning from the march on Moscow.

When he got tired of singing, Schweik sat down on a

pile of gravel, lit his pipe and after having a rest, trudged on towards new adventures.

Rosemary Kavan

FREEDOM AT A PRICE

OUR HOMECOMING, AT the end of 1950, was a
rude shock. We were not prepared for the changed atmosphere. Gone was the exuberance of the liberation year.
People were tight-faced, grim, tired of perpetual shortages.
There was tension in the air. Political differences had
sharpened; society was once more divided. Arrests had been

---

*Rosemary Kavan, a middle-class English woman, moved to Czechoslovakia
with her Communist husband in 1945. The Stalinist purges of the early
fifties stole her husband and her idealism; she became deeply involved in
the Czech underground. This excerpt from her 1985 autobiography,*
Freedom at a Price, *describes their early years.*

made of foreign agents, but also of Czech communists. Among them were Evžen Klinger and Otto Šling whom we had known in London during the war. The Party was probing for further enemies within its ranks. Pavel found the Foreign Ministry veiled in unease.

Karel had inherited our previous flat and we were offered a partly furnished flat in a villa in the best residential part of the Smíchov district, called Na Hřebenkách. It was the epitome of Austro-Hungarian magnificence. (Actually, our flat represented only half of the original apartment, which had extended over the whole of the ground floor.) The rooms were huge and high, light and airy. The floors, made of large squares of highly-polished mahogany, glowed redly. Into the panelled walls were laid glass cabinets for the display of precious porcelain. From the ceilings hung enormous chandeliers, comprising hundreds of droplets, glistening like tears in sunshine. The whole of one wall of the central room was windowed and looked out on a garden of trees, grass and shrubs. In front of the window extended a vast oak desk, intricately carved and matching the imposing fireplace in the adjacent room, which was separated by tall, oak doors.

My legs buckled under me and I had a premonition as I sank into a velvet seat attached to the wall panelling. Give this no more than eighteen months, I told myself.

A few days later the first blow fell. Pavel was eating his dinner in silence. It was not his usual animated silence, in which problems were propelled back and forth, unripe ideas were shunted into sidings and fruitful solutions were sent up the main track into the morrow. It was a void, oppressive silence.

"Is there anything—" I was about to say "wrong", but that might have provoked merely an irritated denial, so I substituted "new"?

"Mm, yes. A regulation has been brought out. Employees with Western wives have to leave the Ministry."

"Do you mean you are getting the sack because of the geographical accident of my birth?"

"Yep. It isn't a question of loyalty—you had a very good report from the Embassy—but of security," Pavel soothed me. "Actually, in my case, notice is not to take effect immediately. I am to complete some major projects before I go."

Pavel's indefinite notice dragged on and he continued working with the sword of Damocles hanging over his head, a state of insecurity that was not exactly what his London doctor had recommended.

Having unexpectedly been converted into a liability, I was eager to prove that a bourgeois background was no obstacle to honest toil. Without telling Pavel, I went to the headquarters of the Women's Union and told them I wanted to work in heavy industry, the heavier the better. The clerk arranged a six-month temporary job at the Tatravagonka engineering works, which produced trams and train wagons. Pavel's reaction was as dispiriting as I had anticipated. "Don't be absurd! You can't operate a machine, you're notoriously cackhanded. Even the egg-whisk falls apart in your hand. You'll probably maim yourself for life, and where will that leave your family?"

I declined to consider that possibility.

At four thirty in the morning the screech of the alarm woke me. I arrived at the factory gate at ten minutes to six and was directed to the cadre department; there I was told to report to comrade Králík in shop 620. Comrade Králík was standing hands behind his back, surveying his domain. His figure bulged under the faded blue coat. His name by an oversight was Rabbit; it should clearly have been Pig. (I had in mind, of course, a clean, socialist porker.) Small, darting eyes and a snub nose clustered in the centre of a wide expanse of pink flesh, flanked by large red ears standing out at right angles.

"Ha, another of you come to expiate your sins!" was his discouraging greeting. I flinched. In a sense he was right, but not entirely. I explained that all I wanted was to do some useful work at grassroots level. Králík shrugged. "We'll put you on Technical Control. They need another hand and you can't do much harm there. Follow me."

He led me through the shop, a cheerless building. The air was warm, and heavy with dust and metal particles. The dingy, biscuit-coloured walls were like the tear-smudged face of a grubby infant. The high, mottled windows streaked the concrete floor with dirty light; puddles of yellowy-brown liquid lay around. The machines from which the liquid trickled were a dark greenish-brown.

Striding ahead, Králík threw remarks over his shoulder. "You'll find life here a bit different from what you're used to. I'm a disciplinarian. Six o'clock sharp the operatives are at their machines and you'll be in your pen. If you clock in late that means a day off your holiday. You've a quarter-of-an-hour for lunch in the canteen any time between eleven and two. That's generous. At other factories lunch is taken after the shift."

We reached a small pen presided over by a school-marmish woman assisted by a dark and lively girl.

Králík introduced me. "Show her the ropes, Comrade Horská, and keep a sharp look out for sabotage. You can't trust these foreign elements." He left chuckling.

Comrade Horská spoke slowly and loudly as though all foreigners were congenital idiots: "Every worker brings the first piece of every batch to us for checking. If we pass an incorrect measurement, all the parts in the batch will be inaccurate. If they cannot be adjusted, they go for scrap and the batch has to be machined again. You must be careful when counting the batches. If a batch is short, assembly is held up until the missing pieces are machined. All these precious hours can never be retrieved, and may mean the failure of the factory plan." Luba, the younger woman, laughed good naturedly: "Anka thinks socialism begins and ends at this counter."

A worker brought me a pin to inspect.

"This pin is three millimetres short," I pointed out diffidently.

"Christ, that's nothing to do with me!" was the polite rejoinder. "I get 'em like that, see, I'm a driller. I only want to know is the distance from head to hole correct and is the ruddy hole the right size? The tapering pin goes in here, see. And holds the pin in place. It doesn't matter if it sticks out half-a-metre beyond." He went off muttering: "Don't know a pin from a knitting needle."

Luba remarked dryly: "Železný's soon forgotten that not so long ago he knew as much about drilling as he did about bear-keeping."

After a substantial lunch in the canteen, Železný fell into step beside me.

"Where'd they direct you from?"

"I beg your pardon?"

"Who gave you the push?"

"No one, I wasn't employed before."

"Oh, I thought you were a formerly."

"A formerly?"

"A former teacher, lawyer, researcher and so on."

"No, this is my first job."

"Got the wrong pedigree, eh? Father had his own business?"

"Good heavens, no!"

"Is he German? You've got a bit of an accent."

"No, English."

"Ah, that explains it. Your husband fought in the West and this is the only kind of work you can get. Don't let it worry you; there's thousands of us. General sort of swop over. The highly qualified professional people are laying roads, building bridges and operating machines, and the dumb clots—whose fathers used to dig, sweep or brick-lay—are on top, telling the others where to lay the roads, what to produce and how to spend the country's money. The consequence is the roads look like ploughed fields, we make things we can't sell and the bridges can't be used for traffic. There's one called the Bridge of the Intellectuals over the Vltava at Bráník built by doctors of law. The bridge is all right, but the dolts in the top drawer forgot to plan a road leading to and from it! Then they wonder why the economy is going downhill like a ten-ton lorry with the brakes off."

There was an India rubber quality about Mr. Železný. He was round; he bounced as he walked; his face slipped into a variety of cheerful grimaces. He looked as though he would rebound to safety if he were dropped off the top of a cliff.

Having found an audience, albeit an incredulous one,

Mr. Železný continued: "I'm here under the Desk-to-Bench campaign. 'Too many fat backsides warming too many office stools. We need more hands at the bench, the seam and the furnace,' they said. Seventy-seven thousand of us were re-directed.

"I'm not complaining about the job: I don't earn less. It's the principle I object to. First, I don't take kindly to being directed; second, this is a waste of good will and good people. What industry needs to increase productivity is more qualified technicians and engineers, not clerks, artisans and judges.

"The joke is, a Party member gets to be foreman, supervisor or such and goes bonkers over a lot of papers he can't get the hang of, and the works gets flooded with half-a-million screws and not a nut in the place, except the one behind the desk. Am I boring you?"

"No, no. It's very interesting."

"Well, you see that tall lanky miller with specs. Looks

standoffish? That's Dr. Brugel. He was de-actionized."

"Paralysed?""Not exactly. Put out of action by an Action Committee in 1948. They were set up to purge the reactionaries, or that was the general idea; but hit a Czech, particularly a communist Czech with an idea, and he'll swallow it hook, line and sinker, plus the bloke at the other end, if you get me. They sorted out everyone who they decided was a potential menace: Catholics, Sokolites, ex-Scouts. Brugel was a lawyer. The legal profession caught it good and proper. The lawyer's job is to protect the individual, so where the individual hasn't got any rights, it's a waste of good money paying lawyers, isn't it? They said: 'Sign or get out!' and stuck an application to join the CP under his nose. But Brugel had principles. 'I'm a Catholic; you're atheists,' he said. 'I support your social policy but I cannot join a party that denies God.' So he was declared politically unreliable and flung out on his ear."

I was disturbed by Železný's revelations. I had envisaged a socialism that would eliminate, not generate, injustice. But when I voiced my doubts to Pavel he dismissed them with the axiom: "When you cut down a forest, chips fly."

Rising so early in the morning simply to count other people's products was a disproportionate effort. Despite Pavel's gloomy prognostications, I was determined to get on to a machine. I badgered Králík. One day he came up to the pen, just before the end of the shift and shouted: "Hey, you, Comrade English-woman, there's a batch here wants doing quickly. If you care to stay on, you can have a go."

I followed him with alacrity. Králík gabbled instructions: "The bolt fits here onto this jig; adjust the ends so that the drill passes through the aperture, press the starting button, apply the self-act lever, halfway through raise the drill slightly to release the swarf, switch on again but before the drill penetrates to the outside and scorches, take it through slowly by hand. See that the holes are perfectly perpendicular; this batch is for a job that's going to the Soviet Union. And—er—take care. You know the Czech saying: 'Clumsy flesh has to go!' "

With my courage like a lump of cheese in my throat, I gingerly set the machine going. I had reckoned without the jet of suds. Suddenly, it became afflicted with a nervous twitch and poured its obnoxious liquid into my boot. What did I do first: stop the machine or quell the jet? Mistakenly I grabbed the jet. There was a noise like sizzling bacon and blue smoke rose from the drill hole. I stopped the machine and tried to lift the lever. The drill was stuck faster than Carver Doone in the bog.

"Well, how's it going?" Králík's gentle bass boomed in my ear.

Humbly I explained about the jet.

"Let's have a look at it," he grunted. "Ježíšmarjá, it only needs the stop-cock tightening at the joint. H'mm it won't grip, worn smooth. Well, tie it up with rag. Use your imagination, girl!"

That was the last piece of advice I had expected to be given on the shop floor. Králík separated the drill from the machine. "Take the jig over to the locksmiths. They'll get the drill out for you. They've got the right tools."

I staggered off to the locksmiths under the crushing weight of the jig. Ten minutes later I was back at work with a newly-ground drill and the conviction that this would be my first and last set of holes for the construction of communism.

The rest of the batch went without mishap. There were only three pieces left. My confidence rose above the plimsoll line, then the machine let out an ear-jarring shriek. The lever was free. I set the drill twirling again. A second screech. I put the bolt aside and finished the remaining two.

"That was a pip in the steel," Králík explained. "Very bad for the drills."

And for the nerves, I added silently. I braced myself. "May I carry on tomorrow?"

Králík hesitated, then said: "All right, you can stay on while Mlýnek is off sick."

"For Chrissake, what are you doing, Bek, you clumsy ox?" Our supervisor's angry voice sounded above the din early the following morning. "This pile's millimetres out."

Bek, a tubby turner, retorted: "The first piece was okay—Technical Control passed it. Something must have come loose in this old bag of tricks."

"It was in perfect order until you took it over," Králík roared. "If there's anything wrong with it, it's your own damn carelessness, or more likely wilful damage. What can one expect from a former hotel-keeper? You've lost your own business, now you're ruining ours. From now on, you're off machining and on sweeping."

After the shift I went to look for Táborský, an elderly, taciturn fitter.

"Would you do me a favour, comrade."

"Ugh, what?"

"Would you look at the machine Bek's been using?"

The fitter gazed at me through shaggy eyebrows that grew over his eyes like a Sealyham terrier's, concealing his thoughts more thoroughly than his clamped lips. He slowly raised an eyebrow and revealed one brown eye, in which there was a glint of something—could it be understanding? He nodded. Then he went over to the machine, examined it and tried it out.

"Inaccurate," he pronounced.

"Could the defect have been caused by careless treatment?"

"Could've—over many years."

"But that little chap, Bek, had only been on it three months."

"Mm, machine's got to wear out some time. This one's pretty old. Needs a thorough overhaul."

"Then why isn't that done?"

"I'm only the fitter for two shops. The supervisors won't allot sufficient time for machine maintenance, especially when they're running two or three shifts. It's pretty general. It'll catch up on them in the long run, though. Then, instead of expanding capital goods production, they'll be replacing what's got worn out through neglect."

This was an unusually long speech for Táborský. I pressed my point: "So it can't be proved that Bek was to blame?"

"Nope."

"Couldn't you get him reinstated?"

He looked at me suspiciously.

"I'm not interested in him as a man or a class symbol. I just don't like injustice."

Táborský waved his hand, gesturing at his many years in a patently unjust world. "I'm not risking a head-on clash with Králík after all these years," he replied.

"But?"

"You're young, you're new, you take everything a sight too seriously. I don't know why I should bother but I'll do this: I'll speak to the supervisor in 420. That's my other shop and that's where Bek is sweeping now. The supervisor is reasonable; he can put Bek onto a machine there."

"Thanks."

"Ugh."

Just before lunch Táborský passed my machine. He nodded; he had kept his promise.

At 2:15 P.M. the morning shift crowded into Králík's office for the monthly trade union meeting. Králík opened with a critical attack on 620's standards. Quality was being sacrificed to quantity. "Comrades, we are not going to build socialism on rejects," he cried. "Last year rejects cost our works two million crowns. This year there has been an improvement but it's still not good enough. The youngsters are the worst offenders. You've had it easy," he thundered. "You've given up nothing to achieve power, working-class power. We old communists had to risk our lives and liberties for what is yours by right under the Constitution. Bullets, baton charges and the inside of a prison cell were the answers we got to demands for work and a living wage."

Luba muttered: "Here we go again. Bloody Wednesday and all that. We can't help not having been born and shot at during the First Republic."

Pulkrábek, another turner, spoke up: "The Party can't live on its past. We've got to solve present problems. We're a long way from communism and reward according to need. In the meanwhile we've got families to feed. Instead of speechifying, why don't you come up with some useful ideas for avoiding rejects? It's not only the prestige of 620 and your bonus that are at stake, but our takings too. We don't exactly jump for joy when we have to machine a second batch for nothing."

Železný put in: "All it wants is for every worker to be issued with a Vernier gauge."

"Where the hell will the money come from?" Králík growled.

"So he can check on his work periodically," Železný went on, unperturbed. "Or for you to go the rounds two or three times a shift."

"Are you telling me how to run my shop, you ink-blotter?" Králík blustered.

"It's reasonable what Železný says," broke in fifteen-stone Tonda who operated four centre lathes. If there was one man whom Králík respected, it was Tonda. Other voices murmured approval.

"Okay, okay, I'll do my best." Králík could shift weight swiftly when the majority closed ranks against him. "Comrade Mastná, put down in the minutes: Comrade Králík: socialist pledge: to make several extra rounds of inspection per shift with a view to reducing rejects. Send a copy to the Works Committee."

Having adroitly turned the situation to his own advantage, Králík brought up the next item—delays in deliveries of material. The ball was kicked from Bartoň to Jarmila, the delivery girl, to Králík, from workshop to workshop, from factory to steel works and from there to the raw material suppliers and finally ended up at Ostrava waiting for vacant goods wagons.

"We've been through all this umpteen times," a weary borer grumbled. Then someone else complained that workers were not paid for time lost through inefficient planning. This brought forth a tirade from Králík on production cost and lack of political consciousness. The situation was obviously aggravated by Králík's inability to foresee and forestall hitches. No one accused him outright for, I gathered, he tended to revenge himself on his critics by allotting them the least profitable batches. The argument died down among angry shrugs.

Králík announced a new check by the rate fixers. As this would inevitably lead to some hardening of norms, it met with resistance.

"We'll never increase productivity otherwise," said Králík. "Figures here show that the works as a whole wastes fifteen per cent of its working time. Workers don't start promptly; they extend snack and lunch breaks and many are at the clocking machines, washed and ready to leave, at two P.M. Full utilization of your eight hours will counter-balance speeded-up operations."

This was a very different picture from the propaganda in the official Czech press, which presented soaring productivity, exceeded targets and cosy concord between floor and management. The factory seemed to be divided into those who were driving themselves to the limits of endurance for what they believed in, and those who took advantage of the shortage of labour to do as little as possible for as much as possible.

However, when Králík appealed for a Sunday shift to complete an order for the Soviet Union, which was behind schedule, there was no lack of volunteers. During the shift carping and discontent were forgotten.

WHEN MLÝNEK RETIRED on a disability pension I was transferred to the permanent payroll. At the end of my second week as a full-blown driller, Pulkrábek came up to me with the words: "Bartoň says would you mind dashing this job off; it's part of a batch that's already gone forward. This box got forgotten."

The box was the standard type, with a green job card tucked down one side. But my early warning system was functioning. I glanced warily inside. A dark mass met my eye. An old trick! Fortunately, though a large spider will send me into hysterics, the genus *rattus* has never caused my to flutter. I pulled the dead rat out by its tail, and handed it and the job card back to Pulkrábek, saying: "Please return this to Comrade Bartoň and tell him the size of the hole hasn't been specified."

The young man grinned. Stifled laughter echoed round the shop. I had passed my ordeal. Thereafter the shop addressed me by the familiar "thou."

Friday was pay day. On this particular Friday I unfolded my slip and read 1500 crowns. Impossible! I went to Bartoň and asked to see the job books.

"Why?" he growled suspiciously.

"I think there's been a mistake."

"If you've got too little, you'll have to put more effort into it next week. I've been on this job twenty years and I've never forgotten to book a job."

I said gently: "Comrade Bartoň, I've been over-paid not underpaid."

His mouth dropped open as though his jaw had become dislocated.

"Then what are you complaining about?"

"I want to put the accounts right."

"You must be joking! Well, if you insist, it's 102's business."

The clerk there told me that no discrepancy had been discovered. He winked. "Have a drink on me and forget it."

I protested: "I don't want to take socialist money I haven't earned. If everyone took home a few hundred crowns that weren't covered by goods produced, what would happen to the economy?"

He burst out laughing. "My dear innocent, you shouldn't worry your little head about a paltry couple of hundred, if you knew how much material people smuggle home every week. There's hardly a man of them hasn't put together a washing machine out of snaffled parts."

I couldn't believe my ears. Workers stealing under socialism!

I spotted a book labelled 620 and went through the items. Here was an error—a small batch of pins: 480 instead of 48, and farther down 25 plates for 300 instead of 30. "There you are!" I crossed off the offending noughts.

"What are you doing to my books, young woman?" He wailed. "I'll have to recast my figures and it's ten minutes to two." He was outraged at having to put in a few moments' overtime on account of my eccentric integrity.

I asked Tonda, who was a communist, whether it was true that parts were taken out of the factory, hoping he would deny it. But he confirmed that this was so.

"But that's stealing!"

Tonda scratched his head. "I doubt if the men see it like that. We own the means of production, don't we? So we can't steal what belongs to us?"

"As far as appropriating parts is concerned, the factory belongs to the workers," I persisted, "But when it comes to decisions of management, they don't feel it's theirs?"

Tonda was too honest to wriggle out of the question. "No, maybe they don't—consciously. But they'd defend it with their lives if the capitalists tried to take it back." He changed the subject. "By the way, a party of us are going for a beer; we usually do on Fridays. Care to come along?"

Never in my life had I managed to get through a whole pint of beer, but if he'd asked me to share a cup of hemlock, I wouldn't have refused.

It was a poky little pub with smoke-blackened walls and ceiling. The beer was served in litre tankards. And it wasn't even gravity English bitter but a full-bodied ten. The waitress, of welterweight dimensions, wielded five full tankards in each hand. I needed two hands to lift one. "Do or die," I muttered and sent down half at one lift of the elbow.

Tonda produced an accordion and we all burst into song. Czech folk songs are so delightfully tuneful that not even hectolitres of flowing hops and malt can drown their inherent musicality. The repertoire is inexhaustible: if you were to ride round the world on a penny-farthing bicycle, singing non-stop, you would still have some over for an encore.

Further tankards appeared before me; my new status as a member of the labouring fraternity precluded refusal. Summoning the remnants of my willpower, which were floating in Pilsen's famous liquid, I downed several more.

"That's my girl!" Tonda rumbled.

"I dunno so much about that," Železný grinned, looking me up and down in my usual slacks and sloppy sweater. "Looks like they ran short of material when they assembled Ros: if it weren't for her nose, you couldn't tell whether she was coming or going."

This raised a general laugh. In another land at another time, I might have made a fortune as a predecessor of

Twiggy; as it was, I had to stand up to some goodnatured teasing, for the average Czech man likes his pound of flesh.

When I stood up to go home, the pub tilted like a boat on the Mácha lake in a squall.

"I'll see you home, nipper," Tonda offered.

He delivered me to my doorstep and rang the bell. Pavel appeared.

"Your wife, Comrade Doctor," Tonda announced. "She'll be all right after a good sleep."

I endeavoured to draw myself up to a dignified height and step over my threshold. Instead, deprived of my support, I collapsed into Pavel's arms and blissful slumber.

Milan Kundera

THE BOOK OF LAUGHTER
AND FORGETTING

IN FEBRUARY 1948, Communist leader Klement Gottwald stepped out on the balcony on a Baroque palace in Prague to address the hundreds of thousands of his fellow citizens packed into Old Town Square. It was a crucial moment in Czech history—a fateful moment of the kind that occurs once or twice in a millennium.

Gottwald was flanked by his comrades, with

Novelist Milan Kundera is the author of six genre-melding novels, which combine Czech and Slovak political history, comic asides, essays on erotic matters, and good stories. This excerpt is from his 1980 masterpiece, The Book of Laughter and Forgetting.

Clementis standing next to him. There were snow flurries, it was cold, and Gottwald was bareheaded. The solicitous Clementis took off his own fur cap and set it on Gottwald's head.

The Party propaganda section put out hundreds of thousands of copies of a photograph of that balcony with Gottwald, a fur cap on his head and comrades at his side, speaking to the nation. On that balcony the history of Communist Czechoslovakia was born. Every child knew the photograph from posters, schoolbooks, and museums.

Four years later Clementis was charged with treason and hanged. The propaganda section immediately air-brushed him out of history and, obviously, out of all the photographs as well. Ever since, Gottwald has stood on that balcony alone. Where Clementis once stood, there is only bare palace wall. All that remains of Clementis is the cap on Gottwald's head.

IT IS 1971, and Mirek says that the struggle of man against power is the struggle of memory against forgetting.

That is his attempt to justify what his friends call carelessness: keeping a careful diary, preserving all correspondence, taking notes at meetings where there is discussion of the current situation and debate of where to go from here. Nothing we do is in violation of the constitution, he tells them. Trying to hide, feeling guilty—that's the beginning of the end.

A week ago, while working with a crew on the roof of a new building, he looked down and had a sudden dizzy spell. He lost his balance and grabbed at a poorly fastened beam, but it came loose and he had to be pulled out from under it. At first the injury looked serious, but later, when he learned it was just a run-of-the-mill broken arm, he said to himself with satisfaction that now he'd get a week or two off and have time for some things he'd been meaning to take care of.

He had finally come around to the position of his

more cautious friends. True, the constitution guaranteed freedom of speech; but the law punished any act that could be construed as undermining the state. Who could tell when the state would start screaming that this or that word was undermining it? He decided he'd better put the incriminating papers in a safe place after all.

First, though, he wanted to settle the Zdena problem. He called her long distance, but couldn't reach her. He wasted four whole days calling. Then yesterday he'd finally gotten through. She'd promised to wait for him this afternoon.

His seventeen-year-old son protested that he couldn't possibly drive with his arm in a cast. It really was pretty hard going. His injured arm swung helpless and useless in its sling on his chest. Whenever he changed gears, he had to let go of the steering wheel for a second.

TWENTY-FIVE YEARS had gone by since his affair with Zdena, and all he had left of it was a few memories.

Once she showed up dabbing her eyes with a handkerchief and blowing her nose. He asked her what the matter was. A Russian statesman had died the day before, she told him. Some Zhdanov, Arbuzov, or Masturbov. Judging by the number of teardrops, she was more disturbed by Masturbov's death than by the death of her own father.

Could that actually have happened? Or was her lament for Masturbov merely a figment of his present hatred? No, it *had* happened, though of course the immediate circumstances making the event credible and real escaped him now, and the memory had become implausible, a caricature.

All his memories of her were like that. They had taken a tram back from the apartment where they made love for the first time. (Mirek was particularly gratified to note that he had completely forgotten their copulations, couldn't conjure up a single second of them.) Bumping up and down in a corner seat, she looked gloomy, introspective, amazingly old. When he asked her why she was so withdrawn, she told him she hadn't been satisfied with their lovemaking. She said he'd made love to her like an intellectual.

In the political jargon of the day "intellectual" was an expletive. It designated a person who failed to understand life and was cut off from the people. All Communists hanged at the time by other Communists had that curse bestowed upon them. Unlike people with their feet planted firmly on the ground, they supposedly floated in air. In a sense, then, it was only fair they have the ground pulled out from under them once and for all and be left there hanging slightly above it.

But what did Zdena mean when she accused him of making love like an intellectual?

For one reason or another she hadn't been satisfied with him, and just as she was capable of imbuing an abstract relationship (her relationship to a stranger like Masturbov) with the most concrete of feelings (in the form of tears), she could give the most concrete of acts an abstract meaning and her dissatisfaction a political name.

LOOKING INTO THE rearview mirror, he realized that a car had been tailing him all along. He had never had any doubt he was being followed, but so far they had acted with masterly discretion. Today a radical change had taken place: they wanted him to know about them.

In the middle of some fields about fifteen miles outside Prague there was a tall fence with a car-repair shop behind it. He had a good friend there and needed him to replace a faulty starter. He pulled up to the entrance. It was blocked by a red-and-white-striped gate. A heavy woman was standing beside it. Mirek waited for her to raise the gate, but she just stared at him, motionless. He honked his horn, but got no response. He looked out the window. "Not behind bars yet?" asked the woman.

"No, not yet," answered Mirek. "How about raising the gate?"

She looked at him impassively for a few more long seconds, then yawned, went over to the gatekeeper's cabin, dropped into a desk chair, and turned her back on him.

So he got up out of the car, walked around the gate, and went into the service area to look for his friend the mechanic. The mechanic came back with him. He raised the gate himself (the woman was still sitting impassively in the cabin), and Mirek drove his car in.

"That's what you get for showing off on television," said the mechanic. "Every broad in the country knows what you look like."

"Who is she?" Mirek asked.

He learned that the invasion of Czechoslovakia by Russian troops, which had made themselves felt everywhere, had changed her life as well. Seeing that people in higher places (and everyone was higher than she was) were being deprived of power, status, employment, and daily bread on the basis of the slightest allegation, she got all excited and started denouncing people herself.

"Then how come she's still working the gate? Haven't they even promoted her?"

The mechanic smiled. "They can't. She doesn't know how to count to five. All they can do is let her go on with her denunciations. That's her only reward." He raised the hood and peered inside at the engine.

Mirek was suddenly aware of someone a few steps away. He turned and saw a man in a gray jacket, white shirt and tie, and brown slacks. His strong neck and bloated face were topped by a shock of artificially waved gray hair. He stood there watching the mechanic leaning under the raised hood.

After a while the mechanic noticed him too. "Looking for somebody?" he asked, straightening up.

"No," answered the man with the strong neck and wavy hair. "I'm not looking for anybody."

The mechanic leaned down over the engine again and said, "Right in the middle of Prague, Wenceslaus Square, there's this guy throwing up. And this other guy comes along, takes a look at him, shakes his head, and says, 'I know just what you mean.' "

THE BLOODY MASSACRE in Bangladesh quickly covered over the memory of the Russian invasion of Czechoslovakia, the assassination of Allende drowned out the groans of Bangladesh, the war in the Sinai Desert made people forget Allende, the Cambodian massacre made people forget Sinai, and so on and so forth until ultimately everyone lets everything be forgotten.

In times when history still moved slowly, events were few and far between and easily committed to memory. They formed a commonly accepted *backdrop* for thrilling scenes of adventure in private life. Nowadays, history moves at a brisk clip. A historical event, though soon forgotten, sparkles the morning after with the dew of novelty. No longer a backdrop, it is now the *adventure* itself, an adventure enacted before the backdrop of the commonly accepted banality of private life.

Since we can no longer assume any single historical event, no matter how recent, to be common knowledge, I must treat events dating back only a few years as if they were a thousand years old. In 1939, German troops marched into Bohemia, and the Czech state ceased to exist. In 1945, Russian troops marched into Bohemia, and the country was once again declared an independent republic. The people showed great enthusiasm for Russia—which had driven the Germans from their country—and because they considered the Czech Communist Party its faithful representative, they shifted their sympathies to it. And so it happened that in February 1949 the Communists took power not in bloodshed and violence, but to the cheers of about half the population. And please note: the half that cheered was the more dynamic, the more intelligent, the better half.

Yes, say what you will—the Communists were more intelligent. They had a grandiose program, a plan for a brand-new world in which everyone would find his place. The Communists' opponents had no great dream; all they had was a few moral principles, stale and lifeless, to patch up the tattered trousers of the established order. So of course the grandiose enthusiasts won out over the cautious compromisers and lost no time turning their dream into reality: the creation of an idyll of justice for all.

Now let me repeat: *an idyll, for all.* People have always aspired to an idyll, a garden where nightingales sing, a realm of harmony where the world does not rise up as a stranger against man nor man against other men, where the world and all its people are molded from a single stock and the fire lighting up the heavens is the fire burning in the hearts of men, where every man is a note in a magnificent Bach fugue and anyone who refuses his note is a mere black dot, useless and meaningless, easily caught and squashed between the fingers like an insect.

From the start there were people who realized they lacked the proper temperament for the idyll and wished to leave the country. But since by definition an idyll is one world for all, the people who wished to emigrate were implicitly denying its validity. Instead of going abroad, they went behind bars. They were soon joined by thousands and tens of thousands more, including many Communists, such as Foreign Minister Clementis, the man who lent Gottwald his cap. Timid lovers held hands on movie screens, marital infidelity received harsh penalties at citizens' courts of honor, nightingales sang, and the body of Clementis swung back and forth like a bell ringing in the new dawn for mankind.

And suddenly those young, intelligent radicals had the strange feeling of having sent something into the world, a deed of their own making, which had taken on a life of its own, lost all resemblance to the original idea, and totally ignored the originators of the idea. So those young, intelligent radicals started shouting to their deed, calling it back, scolding it, chasing it, hunting it down. If I were to write a novel about that generation of talented radical thinkers, I would call it *Stalking a Lost Deed*.

THE MECHANIC SHUT the hood, and Mirek asked him how much he owed him.

"Zilch," said the mechanic.

Mirek got behind the wheel. He was touched. He had no desire whatsoever to go on with his trip. He would rather have stayed with the mechanic and swapped jokes. The mechanic leaned over into the car and slapped him on the shoulder. Then he went back to the gate and raised it.

As Mirek drove by, the mechanic made a motion with his head in the direction of a car parked in front of the repair-shop entrance.

The man with the thick neck and wavy hair was leaning up against the open car door, watching Mirek. So was the man behind the wheel. Both of them were brazen and shameless about it, and Mirek tried to return their expression driving past.

He kept an eye on them in the rearview mirror and saw the man jumping into the front seat and the car making a U-turn so they could continue to follow him.

It occurred to him that he should have done something about getting rid of those incriminating papers. If he'd gotten it out of the way the first day of his sick leave and not waited to talk to Zdena, he'd have had a better chance of pulling it off safely. But he couldn't keep his mind off Zdena. He'd been planning to go see her for several years now. But in recent weeks he had the feeling he couldn't put it off anymore, his time was running out, and he'd better do everything possible to make it perfect and beautiful.

BREAKING UP WITH Zdena in those far-removed days (their affair had lasted almost three years) filled him with a feeling of boundless freedom, and suddenly everything seemed to go right for him. Soon he married a woman whose beauty gave his self-esteem a big boost. Then she died, and he was left alone with his son in a kind of coquettish solitude that attracted the admiration, interest, and solicitude of many other women.

He had also been highly successful in his research, and that shielded him. Since the state needed him, he could afford to make cutting political remarks before anyone else dared to. As the faction trying to recall the deed gained in influence, he began appearing more and more often on television, and before long he had become a well-known personality. When, after the Russians came, he refused to disavow his opinions, they removed him from his job and surrounded him with undercover agents. He remained undaunted. He was in love with his fate and found pomp and beauty in the march to ruin.

Now don't misunderstand me. I said he was in love with his fate, not with himself. Those are two very different things. His life assumed a separate identity and started pursuing interests of its own, quite apart from Mirek's. That is what I mean when I say his life became his fate. Fate had no intention of lifting a finger for Mirek (for his happiness, security, good spirits, or health), whereas Mirek was willing to do everything for his fate (for its grandeur, lucidity, beauty, style, and scrutability). He felt responsible for his fate, but his fate felt no responsibility for him.

He had the same attitude to his life as a sculptor to his statue or a novelist to his novel. One of a novelist's inalienable rights is to be able to rework his novel. If he takes a dislike to the beginning, he can rewrite it or cross it out entirely. But Zdena's existence deprived Mirek of his prerogative as an author. Zdena insisted on remaining part of the opening pages of the novel. She refused to be crossed out.

WHY WAS HE so ashamed of her, anyway?

The most obvious explanation was that very early in the game Mirek had joined forces with those who vowed to hunt down their own deed, while Zdena had always remained loyal to the garden where nightingales sing. More recently she had even joined the two percent of the population who welcomed the Russian tanks.

True, but I don't find it convincing enough. If the only problem was that she had welcomed the Russian tanks, he would simply have given her a good loud public talking-to; he would not have denied ever having known her. No, Zdena had done him a far greater wrong: she was ugly.

But that couldn't make any difference. He hadn't slept with her for more than twenty years.

It made a big difference. Even from so far away Zdena's big nose cast a shadow over his life.

A few years ago he had a beautiful mistress. Once she visited the town where Zdena lived, and came back upset. "How in the world could you have had anything to do with that awful woman?"

He claimed to have known her only casually and categorically denied ever being intimate with her.

Apparently, he was not totally ignorant of one of life's great secrets: women don't look for handsome men, they look for men with beautiful women. Having an ugly mistress is therefore a fatal error. Mirek did his best to do away with all traces of Zdena, and since the nightingale lovers hated him more and more, he hoped that Zdena, making her energetic way up the bureaucratic ladder, would be only too glad to forget him.

He was wrong. She would speak about him anywhere, everywhere, at the drop of a hat. Once by unfortunate coincidence they met at a social event, and she quickly made it clear by referring to past events that she had been intimate with him.

He was furious.

"If you hate her so much, why did you have an affair with her?" a mutual friend once asked him.

Mirek's explanation was that he'd been a twenty-year-old brat at the time, seven years younger than she. Besides, she was respected, admired, omnipotent! She knew practically everyone on the Central Committee! She helped him, pushed him, introduced him to influential people!

"I was a go-getter, man! Understand?" he shouted.

"An aggressive, young go-getter. That's why I hung onto her. I didn't give a damn how ugly she was!"

MIREK WAS NOT telling the truth. Even though Zdena did cry over Masturbov's death, she had no influential contacts twenty-five years ago and was in no position to further her own career, to say nothing of anyone else's.

Then why did he make it all up? Why did he lie?

Mirek was steering with one hand. Looking up at the rearview mirror, he saw the agents' car, and suddenly blushed. A completely unexpected memory had just surfaced.

After she reproached him for acting too much like an intellectual that first time they made love, he wanted to set things right and give her a demonstration of spontaneous, unbridled passion. So it wasn't true he'd forgotten all their copulations! This one he could picture quite plainly. He moved on her with feigned frenzy, making a long snarling noise—the kind a dog makes when at war with his master's slipper—and observing her (with mild surprise) stretched out there beneath him so calm, collected, almost indifferent.

The car resounded with that snarl from twenty-five years ago, the agonizing sound of his submissiveness and servile fervor, the sound of his willingness to conform and adapt, his laughable predicament, his misery.

Yes, it's true. Mirek was willing to proclaim himself an ambitious go-getter rather than admit the truth: he'd taken an ugly mistress because he didn't dare go after beautiful women. Zdena was as high as he rated himself then. A weak will and utter poverty—those were the secrets he had hoped to hide.

The car resounded with the furious snarl of passion, trying to convince him that Zdena was merely a phantom to be blotted out if he meant to obliterate his hated youth.

He pulled up in front of her house. The car on his tail pulled up behind him.

HISTORICAL EVENTS USUALLY imitate one another without much talent, but in Czechoslovakia, as I see it, history staged an unprecedented experiment. Instead of the standard pattern of one group of people (a class, a nation) rising up against another, all the people (an entire generation) revolted against their own youth.

Their goal was to recapture and tame the deed they had created, and they almost succeeded. All through the 1960s they gained in influence, and by the beginning of 1968 their influence was virtually complete. This is the period commonly referred to as the Prague Spring: the men guarding the idyll had to go around removing microphones from private dwellings, the borders were opened, and notes began abandoning the score of Bach's grand fugue and singing their own lines. The spirit was unbelievable. A real carnival!

Russia, composer of the master fugue for the globe, could not tolerate the thought of notes taking off on their own. On August 21, 1968, it sent an army of half a million men into Bohemia. Shortly thereafter, about a hundred and twenty thousand Czechs left their country, and of those who remained about five hundred thousand had to leave their jobs for manual labor in the country, at the conveyor belt of an out-of-the-way factory, behind the steering wheel of a truck—in other words, for places and jobs where no one would ever hear their voices.

And just to be sure not even the shadow of an unpleasant memory could come to disturb the newly revived idyll, both the Prague Spring and the Russian tanks, that stain on the nation's fair history, had to be nullified. As a result, no one in Czechoslovakia commemorates the 21st of August, and the names of the people who rose up against their own youth are carefully erased from the nation's memory, like a mistake from a homework assignment.

Mirek's was one of the names thus erased. The Mirek currently climbing the steps to Zdena's door is really only a white stain, a fragment of barely delineated void making its way up a spiral staircase.

Acknowledgments

Excerpt from "Reflections on a Golden City" by Patricia Hampl first appeared in *The New York Times Magazine*. Reprinted by permission of the author.

"Article 202" from *Open Letters: Selected Writings 1965-1990* by Vaclav Havel ©1991 by Paul Wilson. Translated from the Czech by Paul Wilson. Reprinted by permission of Alfred A. Knopf, Inc.

Excerpt from *The Castle* by Franz Kafka ©1954 by Alfred A. Knopf, Inc. Reprinted by permission of Alfred A. Knopf, Inc.

Excerpt from *Utz* by Bruce Chatwin ©1988 by Bruce Chatwin. Reprinted by permission of Viking Penguin Inc.

"Pirates" from *The End of Lieutenant Boruvka* by Josef Skvorecky ©1990 by Paul Wilson. Translated by Paul Wilson. Reprinted by permission of W.W. Norton & Co.

Excerpt from "A Night in Prague" by Janet Malcolm first appeared in *The New Yorker*, November 19, 1990. Reprinted by permission of the author.

Excerpt from *Freedom at a Price* by Rosemary Kavan ©1985 by Jan Kavan. Reprinted by permission of Verso/NLB, London and New York.

Excerpt from *The Book of Laughter and Forgetting* by Milan Kundera ©1980 by Alfred A. Knopf, Inc. Reprinted by permission of Alfred A. Knopf, Inc.